Henry R. Whitehouse

The Sacrifice of a Throne

being an account of the life of Amadeus, duke of Aosta, sometime king of Spain

Henry R. Whitehouse

The Sacrifice of a Throne
being an account of the life of Amadeus, duke of Aosta, sometime king of Spain

ISBN/EAN: 9783337237844

Printed in Europe, USA, Canada, Australia, Japan

Cover: Foto ©Andreas Hilbeck / pixelio.de

More available books at **www.hansebooks.com**

Amadeus I. King of Spain.

THE SACRIFICE OF A THRONE

BEING AN ACCOUNT OF THE LIFE OF

AMADEUS

DUKE OF AOSTA, SOMETIME KING OF SPAIN

BY

H. REMSEN WHITEHOUSE

*Formerly attached to United States Legation at Madrid, Late
Secretary of Legation and Consul General to Central America ;
Secretary of Legation to Mexico, Secretary of the Pan-
American Conference ; and recently Secretary of
United States Embassy to Italy*

———   —

NEW YORK
BONNELL, SILVER & CO.
1897

TO MY WIFE

MARGARET McBURNEY WHITEHOUSE

IN MEMORY

OF HAPPY ROMAN DAYS

I DEDICATE THIS

STUDY.

"BEAU RIVAGE"
    OUCHY, JUNE, 1892.

CONTENTS.

CHAPTER V.

CHAPTER VI.

CHAPTER VII.

CHAPTER VIII.

CHAPTER IX.

PAGE

LIST OF ILLUSTRATIONS.

THE SACRIFICE OF A THRONE.

CHAPTER I.

ON the morning of the thirtieth of May, 1845, the Lady of Honor of the Duchess of Savoy, seeking Charles Albert in the royal palace of Turin, informed His Majesty that his daughter-in-law, Her Royal Highness Maria Adelaide, had just given birth to a prince.

"He is welcome," exclaimed the King, relaxing for a moment from his habitual morose preoccupation. "We will call him Amadeus, and his title shall be Duke of Aosta."

The daughter of the Arch-Duke Ranier,

Viceroy of Lombardy-Venetia, and Princess Elisabeth, sister of the King of Sardinia, Maria Adelaide was consequently closely related by ties of blood to the House of Savoy; being, in fact, her husband's first cousin. Politically an Austrian but born in Milan, she was at heart an Italian and fitted in every respect, as the wife of the Heir to the Throne, to win the sympathy and affections of her future subjects. Eminently pious, yet without bigotry; combining generosity with exquisite tact, the Duchess soon became greatly beloved in Turin where the populace bestowed upon her the title of Providence of the Poor, and where from the date of her marriage (April 13. 1842) to that of her death (January 20, 1855), her gentle and gracious influence greatly added to the popularity and affection of which the princes of the House of Savoy received such ample demonstration.

For purely political reasons there is no doubt that Charles Albert would have preferred a French princess for his daughter-in-law, the project was, however, vigorously combated by the Prime Minister, Count Solaro della Margarita, an old-fashioned and bigoted legitimist, who, as he openly declared, would have burnt **off** his right **hand** sooner than put his signature to a marriage contract by which a descendant of the regicidal Philippe Egalité should enter the House of Savoy.

The "Gazzetta Piemontese" **of May 31,** 1845, contains the following—the first intimation to the public **of** the entrance into the world of one who was **to** play no insignificant **part** on its political stage: "Yesterday at **two in** the afternoon, the Prince just born, on whom it has pleased **H. M.** the King to confer the title of Duke **of Aosta, was privately** baptized by H. E. the Archbishop **in a** chapel expressly prepared **in the** royal apartments."

The Prince was held at the font by his uncle, the Duke **of Genoa.** Salutes were fired, **and** general public rejoicings took place not only in Piedmont but also in the other states of Italy, already turning their eyes towards the little Kingdom at the foot of the Alps, **and** recognizing in its wise and liberal **Princes the** hope of a salvation to come, and the promise of freedom from the chains of foreign bondage.

The title of Duke of Aosta, conferred on **Amadeus by** his royal grandfather, is one of the oldest in the House of Savoy. In 1024 "Humbert **of** the White **Hands**" figures in history with the title of Count of Aosta. The valley has remained ever since the faithful and loyal domain of the family, through vicissitudes and good fortune alike, and a century before Savoy became a Duchy its Princes bore the title of Dukes of Aosta. The castles and palaces of the once powerful de Challant and Roncas families still remain to attest the importance of some of the great vassal houses of the Val d'Aosta.

On the death of Amadeus (January 18, 1890), the title descended, by special decree of King Humbert, to the Prince's eldest son, known up to that time as Emmanuel Philibert, Duke delle Puglie. This young Prince recently married (1895) Princess Helen of Orleans, a lineal descendant of that "regicidal" Philippe Egalité so distasteful to Charles Albert's Prime Minister, Count Solaro della Margarita.

In August, 1864, Prince Amadeus, then barely nineteen years of age, accompanied by Count Guiseppe Pasolini, paid a visit to Aosta and the neighboring towns and villages. The journey, originally planned on account of certain local disturbances which had taken place by reason of the introduction of the Italian language, proved a continual ovation for the

Prince bearing the title of the secluded province. Accustomed to the French tongue, **as** well in private use as in public acts and correspondence, the inhabitants of the valley were profoundly grieved and humiliated when an attempt was made by some over-zealous official **to** force Italian upon them to the total exclusion of their native idiom. Count Pasolini made himself the champion **of** the sturdy mountaineers, and was instrumental in bringing about the visit of the Prince, which effectually **appeased** all hostile feeling and **allayed** the fermentation caused **by the** obnoxious order.

On the evening of the Prince's arrival the municipal body, with all the authorities resid-**ing in Aosta,** solemnly repaired **to** the triumphal arch erected by the Romans to the Emperor Augustus, **there** to receive their Duke, **and to welcome** him with the following address:

"Your Royal Highness:

"It is a great day for the inhabitants of this town, that on which they receive amongst them the son of their magnanimous King, the Prince who bears the name of their country. **On** entering **this ancient city** Your Royal

Highness will find at every step the same hearts as those which, eight hundred years ago, welcomed the chief of your illustrious dynasty, Humbert of the White Hands. Our modest town can certainly not boast of the richness of decoration of the great cities of the Peninsula, but Your Royal Highness will meet here those bronzed mountaineers who on a battle-field know not what retreat means and who are always proud to be enrolled under the banner of the White Cross of Savoy.

"May Your Royal Highness deign to receive the profound homage presented by the municipality of Aosta, in its own name and in the name of this joyful population which has assembled in crowds to contemplate the features of a Prince whom this ancient Duchy will count upon as its most illustrious protector."

This visit of the Prince—described in the enthusiastic local press as restoring to the ancient capital of the Alps the days of its past splendor—fully accomplished the object for which it was undertaken, and caused a revival of fervor and loyalty in the hearts of the simple, honest-minded dwellers of these peaceful regions.

Before Amadeus had attained his third
year Piedmont was fully launched in the Italian movement, and had in fact begun to shape
its destinies. The invasion of the Legations
and the excited state of public feeling in Lombardy and Venetia, together with the increase
of Austrian forces in those provinces, had for
some time made apparent the necessity of
being prepared, and had caused Charles Albert
to make every sacrifice in order that his army
might be in readiness for events which could
not, in the nature of things, be long delayed.
The **death of Pope** Gregory XVI., and **the
amnesty granted to** political offenders by **his
successor, Pius IX., together** with other liberal
acts of the new Pontiff, awoke new hopes.
The patriotic tide swelled **and rolled forward**
in all classes of society and in all **parts of the**
Peninsula. That hot-bed **of political** intrigue
as it had then **become, the salon** of the
Countess Maffei, **in** Milan, teemed **with generous** impulse and the **fervor of martyrdom.
This** famous salon, originally **the** meeting-
place of literary and artistic Italy—not to say
Europe—which began to assemble round the
gifted and charming countess as early as 1834,
continued to **exert its** influence down to **the**
death of **the** hostess in 1886. During **the**

intensely fervent political period extending
from 1849 to 1859, when the struggle for
national independence in Italy was at its
fiercest, the Countess Clara threw herself
heart and soul into the movement, and the
policy of Count Cavour counted amongst the
frequenters of her house some of its staunchest and best known supporters. Balzac,
Verdi, Liszt, Daniel Stern, Aleardi, Manzoni,
and a host of others, celebrated artistic and
poetical lights, now yielded if not the place
of honor at least that of action to men such
as E. Visconti-Venosta (the Italian Arbi-
trator on the recent Behring Sea Commission),
Emilio Dandolo, Massimo d'Azeglio, Emilio
Broglio, and the followers of Count Cavour
and Garibaldi. To the close observer of the
details of the long struggle for Italian independence and unity the records of the subtle
yet persistent influence of the workers revolving round this frail and quiet little lady are
of the greatest interest.

The fall of Louis-Philippe (February 28,
1848) and the declaration of the Republic in
France added fuel to the burning political
passions in Italy. Charles Albert, fully understanding that through the aid of the Liberals alone could he satisfy his noble ambi-

tion of becoming the emancipator of Italy, granted his subjects the constitution so eagerly sought, and swore to maintain it " with the affection of a father and the faith of a King."

While Amadeus, with his brother Humbert and their elder sister, the Princess **Clotilde,** romped about the royal gardens at Turin, **or** the grounds of the castle of Moncalieri, in all the glorious carelessness of healthy childhood, portentous clouds were gathering thick round the throne of their grandfather. Milan **and** Venice had risen to the cry of **" fuori lo** straniero " (away with the foreigner), **and** the Piedmontese were loudly demanding **arms** to aid **their brothers to oust the** Austrian **tyrants.**

On the night of March 25, 1848, an enormous crowd filled the great square before the castle of **Turin.** Silent and calm it awaited the result of the deliberations of the **council of** the King and foremost statesmen of the land. Suddenly the broad windows leading to **the** balcony of the Royal Armory are thrown open and a flood of light inundates the square. The populace awaits breathlessly the appearance of the King, who strides out, the Dukes **of** Savoy and Genoa at his side, waving **a** tricolor flag. The declaration of war—for

such it is—is greeted with an immense
thunder of applause. From this moment the
heart of Italy palpitated in Turin. From that
day the unity, independence and liberty of
Italians was decreed—its fulfilment still, alas!
a question of years of noble sacrifice and
heroic struggle, but henceforth the sacred aim
and unswerving object of whole peoples eager
to become a Nation.

A few days later Charles Albert had crossed
the Ticino with his army and the first brilliant advantages of Pastrengo and Goito had
gladdened the hearts of the patriots, so soon
to be cast down in spite of prodigies of valor
and individual acts of heroism, by the re-
verses of Custoza and Mortara, and the defeat
of Novara. To the advantageous proposals
of peace made by the Austrians through the
English Government, offering to recognize
the independence of Lombardy, including
Peschiera, and granting certain administrative
reforms to Venice, Charles Albert magnani-
mously replied that Italians must all be slaves
or all be free.

After the fateful battle of Novara (March
22, 1849), in which he recognized the loss of
the Italian cause, Charles Albert assembled
his staff around him. In a few touching

words recalling his fidelity to the constitution
and his endeavors to free his fellow-country-
men from the foreign yoke, the King announced his resolution to abdicate in favor
of his son Victor Emmanuel, Duke of Savoy,
in the hope that the new sovereign might be
able to secure better terms, and procure for his
country an honorable peace.

Immediately afterwards the ex-King retired to Oporto, in Portugal, where four
months after his abdication he died of a broken
heart (July 28, 1849). Twenty-four years
later his grandson Amadeus, true to his oath
as constitutional King of Spain, sought the
hospitable soil of Portugal—like his ancestor
a voluntary exile.

Victor Emmanuel II., born July 14, 1820,
was consequently twenty-nine years of age
when the reins of government were so unexpectedly and tragically placed in his hands by
the abdication of his father. Notwithstanding
the crushing responsibilities thrust upon him,
the future Father of his Country manfully accepted the well-nigh hopeless task. It was
urgently necessary to conclude an immediate
armistice and to lay the foundations for an
eventual peace. Marshal Radetzky, however, refused to receive the envoys sent by

Victor Emmanuel, and insisted on treating
with the King in person. Strong in his resolve to accomplish any act of abnegation
necessary for the welfare of his country, the
King bowed beneath this humiliation. The
negotiations for peace were long and difficult. The young King, however, gave proof
of the greatest strength of character, and of
that tireless energy which permeated his whole
nature. Positively refusing to abrogate the
constitution granted by his father, which the
Austrians had looked upon with great dis-
pleasure as a dangerous concession to liberal-
ism, he proudly proclaimed that he preferred
the loss of a thousand crowns, and exile, to
any retraction of the oath by which his father
swore to guard and uphold the liberties
granted to his people. The firmness of the
King and the resolute diplomacy of the new
Prime Minister, Massimo d'Azeglio, finally
succeeded in obtaining for Piedmont (August
6, 1849) conditions of peace considerably
less onerous than might have been feared.

The situation of his country was nevertheless most distressing. The finances exhausted; public credit ruined; the military
organization shattered, and patriotic enthusiasm sadly weakened. Besides financial em-

barrassments, including **a** war indemnity of **seventy-five** millions **of** francs imposed by the victorious Austrians, the government of the **King had** to contend with the animosity of the extremist parties in Parliament, and the continuous venom and hostility **of an** almost unbridled foreign and domestic Press.

Prince Humbert and the Duke of Aosta were respectively in their sixth **and** fifth years when Novara cut short the first brilliant but futile struggle for Italian independence. The death **of** their grandfather Charles Albert in his voluntary exile at Oporto, whither he had retired on his abdication, had **cast a deep gloom over the Court and country, already thrown** into mourning by the recent political disasters. Maria-Theresa, widow **of the late** King, continued **to** reside at the Piedmontese Court, where every delicate attention and loving care were lavished **on** her by **her daughter-in-law,** Maria Adelaide, and the members **of** her family. The rigid etiquette of the late Court, almost Spanish in its methodical inflexibility, was gradually relaxed by Maria Adelaide, and allowed to conform more with the new liberal ideas, assisted by the Queen's own broad views of sentiment and affection. But the dignity of the new sovereign did **not** lose by the contrast. Cheerfully sacrificing all pretension to the rôle of a political woman, she chose in preference that of a tender mother and the gracious protector of those of her subjects most sorely in need of her aid and sympathy. The numerous stories of her unfailing charity and practical assistance in sickness and sorrow among the most humble, give us a clear insight into the simplicity and dignity of the noble woman by whose influence the characters of her children were being formed.

At the time of the accession of Victor Emmanuel the terms of intercourse between parents and their children were very different in Italy from what they have since become, and it required no little moral courage, even in a Queen, to break through deeprooted traditions, and to undertake the radical changes in her own children's education and bearing which she considered as necessary for the growth and maintenance of strong family ties and affection.

Amongst the members of the Piedmontese aristocracy and the upper middle classes the system had been almost one of servitude. Children were taught to consider themselves not as their parents' equals but as their inferiors and subjects. The same marks of humility and subjection were required of them as from actual servants, or as those imposed **by** monastic rules **on** priests towards their superiors. The children addressed their parents in the third person, and were expected to kiss their hands on the rare occasions upon which **they** were admitted into their presence. For the rest the parents abandoned their offspring to the care of servants, or to their tutors, who were generally priests.

Up to the time of her death in 1855, Maria Adelaide carefully watched over and directed the education of her children, faithfully aided **by the** Marchioness Pallavicini di Priola, governess of the **royal** princes. **Victor Emmanuel, however, reserved for** himself **from their** tenderest years **the** supervision **and** strict enforcement **of their** physical training, **and** it is due in **no** mean measure to his **example** and teaching that **the** princes speedily became finished horsemen and keen sportsmen. With Victor Emmanuel the chase was, **to** the end of his life, **an** absorbing passion, **and to** this day his son Humbert yields nothing to him in his enthusiasm. At Aosta there **is a very** characteristic statue representing **Victor** Emmanuel in hunting garb. **The** late King **stands** on a pedestal of rough rocks, his rifle just fallen from the shoulder, a bouquetin expiring at his feet. The bouquetin, extinct in other parts of Europe, is jealously preserved in the royal domain amongst the glaciers and peaks of the Gran Paradiso and Grivola in the Graian Alps. Here invariably, year after year, father and son have spent a few weeks during the summer in the mountain camps, enjoying this splendid but laborious sport.

While thus occupied with the pleasures of home or chase the young King did not allow himself to be careless of the affairs of state, which indeed demanded his constant care and industry. Count Camillo di Cavour had succeeded Massimo D'Azeglio as Prime Minister, and had set himself to the overwhelming task of adjusting the finances and re-ordering the administration of the Kingdom. And the demands were truly appalling, while the means at his disposal were of the most meagre description. The army must be increased; railways must be constructed, and prisons and hospitals be adapted to the exigencies of the times, while the revenues of the state were still further diminished by remissions in taxes and transportation of cereals, made imperious by famine and consequent

suffering and discontent. Yet in spite **of**
harassing cares the young King and his minister were to prove themselves **equal to** the
confidence placed in them by **those who** had
the higher destinies of Italy **at heart.**

CHAPTER II.

COUNT CAVOUR offers one of the greatest examples in history of the broad-minded statesman and crafty diplomatist, combined with the wise and far-seeing administrator and able financier. Patiently pursuing one great aim he neglected none of the small opportunities, or apparently insignificant details, necessary for its accomplishment. This aim was primarily the annexation to the crown of Sardinia of the provinces and duchies of northern Italy, while maturing that greater scheme for the political unity of the Peninsula. This purpose, tirelessly pursued, was the object of his constant pre-occupation and incessant endeavor. The axis around which the whole scheme revolved was, in

Count Cavour's opinion, France; and France then meant Napoleon **the** Third. It was therefore necessary first to win the sympathy of that sovereign and then draw **him** into active participation in Italian affairs; without sacrificing, however, any of the liberties guaranteed by the constitution, or affecting the popularity of **the** King in the other states **of** the Peninsula. The Emperor's theories concerning the rights and principles of nationality were well known. The treaty of Vienna, concluded after **the** fall of **Napoleon I.**, his uncle, and which had **allotted** Lombardy **and Venetia** to Austria, **and** humbled France, was still in force. **By an alliance** with the King of **Piedmont** the double opportunity was offered of paying off an old score, and of righting **a** wrong which was **none** the less burning because long standing.

Count Cavour was not slow **to recognize** the value of such arguments. **From** sentimental argument to action was a long step, yet at Turin it was foreseen. In the Crimean war, apparently a quarrel **having** not the slightest material interest for the little Kingdom at the foot of the Alps, Cavour saw his opportunity. Were Piedmont to bear **her** share of the heat and burden of battle as the

ally of France and England, a place could
hardly be denied her in the concert of European Powers: and this place she coveted
above all else. Futhermore, the friendship
with France could be made to lead eventually
to a cooling off of the amicable relations between France and Austria, and even to a possible rupture between those two countries, of
which Italy would not only be the cause, but
also by which she would prove the gainer.

Through the Piedmontese Ambassador in
Paris, Marquis Villamarina, the fine end of
the wedge was inserted, with the result that
early in December, 1854, the government of
Sardinia was officially invited by France and
England to become a party to the alliance
against Russia. The advantages to accrue to
Sardinia were substantial. Not the least was
a loan made by England of two millions sterling, and the promise that in the negotiations
for peace the sacrifices sustained and services
rendered by Piedmont should be taken into
account. But the clause which best suited
Count Cavour's policy was the stipulation
that Sardinia having entered the European
concert should have a voice in the re-establishment of peace and concerning the political equilibrium of Europe. Nor did Victor

Emmanuel, **once** engaged upon the enterprise, shirk the fulfilment of any of the obligations laid upon him by his allies. The official accounts of the battle of Cernaia teem with praise and admiration of the conduct of the Italian troops, while the fame of General Lamarmora will ever be associated with the **glories** of the campaign.

The character of a prince whose surroundings are permeated with the details of political and military endeavors must necessarily at an early age receive the imprint **of the** events of which he is so close and so interested a spectator. **As** the **son of** an artisan, or manufacturer, will **more** readily turn to matters pertaining **to his** father's **trade, so also** will the mind **of a** King's son earlier **awaken** to a keen appreciation of the science of government, the wheels and machinery of which he sees daily revolving round **him.** We have seen how Maria Adelaide endeavored to cultivate in her children the softening influences of pure family affections and home interests, and these principles **so** lovingly inculcated remained with Amadeus **all** his life long. Yet the stirring events of the first years of their childhood had not **been** without a decided influence on the dispositions

of the two young princes.   They were by race
soldiers ; and upon the death of their mother
their military training was begun in earnest.

The year 1855 was to prove a particularly
sad one for the royal family.

On January 12, the widow of Charles
Albert, Maria Theresa, passed away after a
lingering illness.   Eight days later the King
and his whole country were plunged into
deepest grief and consternation by the death,
in childbed, of Queen Maria Adelaide.   It can
easily be imagined how sincerely the sorrow
of the royal family was shared by the count-
less poor, inhabiting the attics and hovels of
Turin, for whom the charitable Queen had so
long and so generously provided—at what
personal sacrifice only those of her immediate
circle were aware.

An allowance of one hundred thousand
francs, paid quarterly, for dress and personal
expenses, had been made to the Queen at the
time of her marriage.   We are told that
by far the greater part of this was given
away in private charities, and that the Queen
merely expended on her wardrobe the amount
strictly necessary for the maintenance of the
dignity of her position.

Within **three weeks of** the death **of** his **wife,** Victor Emmanuel was still further afflicted by the loss **of** his brother Ferdinand, Duke of Genoa, father of Margherita, present Queen of Italy, **and** of Thomas, the actual Duke.

The relentless demands of public affairs did **not** long allow **Victor** Emmanuel **to** brood over his crushing sorrows. And **perhaps** the ceaseless political activity imposed upon him was the truest relief. Before the close **of** the year 1855 **we** find the King, accompanied by his tireless Minister, **in** Paris **as** the honored **guests of Napoleon III.**

Both from his conversations with the Emperor and leading French statesmen, Count Cavour was satisfied that, should the occasion arise, **his country** might **expect** substantial aid from their powerful **ally.**

After a short visit **to London where the** distinguished Italian visitors **met** with **an** equally cordial reception from **Queen Victoria** and the English public, **the** King returned to Turin.

The Congress of Paris, which assembled **shortly** after this visit, **was** of inestimable **importance to** Piedmont **in so** much as it afforded Cavour the opportunity **of** setting

forth, in an official reunion of the great
European Powers, the wrongs of his countrymen and the unsatisfactory condition of
affairs in the Peninsula. Of course the ty-
rannical governments of the Italian States
under Austrian protection protested against
the unsolicited and unauthorized action of
the Piedmontese statesman. Austria was
especially incensed and loud in her denunciations of any consideration of the subject
by the Congress. But Cavour had had his
say, and a great majority in all parts of Italy
lauded this bold policy to the skies.

Meanwhile the relations between Austria
and Piedmont continued to grow more and
more strained in direct ratio with the increasing cordiality of the French and Italian
rulers.

The popularity of Victor Emmanuel gained
ground year by year as the absolute honesty
and straightforwardness of his policy became
better known. Daniel Manin, the President
of the Venetian Republic of 1848–49, and
Garibaldi, were among the first to rally round
the standard of the King, and to proclaim
their faith in the principle of Italian unity
under the constitutional sceptre of the House
of Savoy. Others who had been the uphold-

ers of the theories of Mazzini followed, and the allegiance of the vast association which was to represent the great Italian national party was assured to Victor Emmanuel.

The Orsini outrage (January **14**, 1858) caused for a time great anxiety to the Piedmontese cabinet, as it was feared the well-founded aspirations, the result of years of patient diplomacy, would be jeopardized, or even irretrievably destroyed. Felix Orsini was a patriot whose whole life had been given up to the Italian cause, and who believed that Napoleon was an obstacle to the realization of his scheme. The crime caused deep consternation throughout Europe, and especially in France. The political world saw in the attempt the handiwork of those secret societies whose ramifications extended over all Italy, and whose aims and objects were currently believed to embrace political assassination. Count Cavour realized the peril of the situation and the necessity of calming the apprehensions of Europe. It was imperatively incumbent on the government to free the state from the insinuations of her enemies, and to clear the holy Italian cause from the discredit involved by the political machina-

3

tions of regicidal fanatics. Combining the
necessities and the opportunities of the crisis
in the most masterly manner, the Prime
Minister addressed a circular to all the King's
representatives abroad, informing them of the
government's interpretation of the unfortunate
situation created by Orsini's crime. After
recording the profound impression produced
in Europe by the outrage, he admits that un-
luckily the authors of the plot were Italians.
The evident aim, he adds, confirmed by the
confession of the guilty principal, was to seek
to provoke by means of the death of the Emperor a revolution in France, and an insurrection in Italy. In view of these attempts, so
frequently renewed, and which all have so
similar an object—namely, a change in the
actual condition of affairs in Italy—one is
forced to ask if in reality there does not exist
in some states of the Peninsula a deep reason
for discontent which it would be to the advantage of all Europe to do away with! The
reason undoubtedly does exist. It is the
result of foreign occupation, principally: it
arises from the corrupt administration of the
Papal States, and the unworthy government
of the Kingdom of Naples. It is the effect of
Austrian preponderance in Italy: the exist-

ence of evils already laid before the Congress
of Paris.

During the summer of this same year
Cavour met the Emperor **Napoleon III. at**
Plombières, and transacted amongst other
political affairs the preliminaries for the marriage between Princess Clotilde, eldest
daughter of his sovereign, and the Emperor's
unruly cousin Prince Napoleon, son **of the**
great Emperor's brother Gerome who had been
King of Westphalia.

Count Cavour certainly had reason **to con-**
gratulate **himself on the results of his policy,**
and the fruit seemed almost within **his grasp**
when, on the occasion of the diplomatic reception **at the Tuileries,** on January **first,** 1859,
Napoleon, after exchanging compliments with
the various foreign Ambassadors, **turned to**
Baron **Hübner, the Austrian Envoy, and**
curtly remarked: "I regret **that the relations**
between France **and Austria are not** as
friendly **as** in the past; but assure your
Emperor that my personal sentiments for him
are unchanged."

European diplomacy was greatly impressed;
and when **a few** days later came reports of
Victor Emmanuel's speech **on** the opening of
the Sardinian **Parliament,** and the publication

in Paris of the pamphlet on Italian affairs, generally accepted as inspired, if not actually written by the Emperor, few doubted that the long-pent storm was to break at last. Commenting on the Emperor's words Lord Cowley wrote to Lord Malmesbury on January 11: " Péreire told the Emperor that his speech to Hübner would cost France a milliard. Added to the King of Sardinia's speech and Prince Napoleon's marriage, it is more likely to cost two."

A few days later the Prince Consort wrote to Baron Stockmar: " The state of Europe has become very perplexed since I last wrote you. Louis Napoleon thinks he has found the right moment for making war, and the right field for it in Italy, and the people about him, especially his cousin, have been constantly dinning into his ears : " C'est une occasion qui ne se trouvera pas une seconde fois aussi belle." . . . The speech on New Year's day seems to have set light to the train before all was ready, and now all Europe is alarmed, and would fain establish a fire brigade. The money market is affected to a degree altogether incredible, and the loss upon the Public Funds in three days is estimated at sixty millions sterling."

The Emperor's words came as a surprise even to Victor Emmanuel and Count Cavour. The latter on reading them smiled, and remarked laconically: "Il paraît que l' Empereur veut aller en avant." Nothing could better have suited the policy of the astute director of the destinies of the Sardinian government. Yet only a month later Victor Emmanuel would seem to have had grave doubts as to the fulfilment of the promises made by his powerful neighbor, who, although personally anxious to redeem his pledges, found himself **confronted by** a hostile public opinion at home which it would have been **dangerous** to ignore.

Driven to bay by the prospect **of a possible abandonment of the** Italian cause, **the** King of Sardinia wrote the Emperor **in the most** urgent terms: **"In** the face **of such an** event," he exclaims, **"which I look upon as** impossible, nothing would be left me **but to** follow the example **of my** father, King Charles Albert, and **to lay down a** crown which I could no longer wear with honor **to** myself **or** with safety for my people. Constrained **to** renounce the throne **of** my ancestors, **what I owe to** myself, **to** the fame of my race, and the welfare **of my coun-**

try, would impose upon me the duty of letting the world know the reasons which had driven me to make so deplorable a sacrifice."

Louis Napoleon was too deeply compromised to withdraw even had his heart not been set on overcoming the difficulties he encountered. It soon became patent that, should an occasion not speedily present, a pretext would be forthcoming to precipitate a crisis.

Meanwhile Piedmont was straining every nerve to prepare for the inevitable struggle, and when the Austrian ultimatum was presented in Turin, its terms were rejected, and diplomatic relations severed on April twenty-sixth, 1859.

CHAPTER III.

ALTHOUGH in order to obtain a clear appreciation of the influence surrounding Prince Amadeus, it has been necessary to attempt in broad outline a sketch of the principal political events of his early years, in which, however, on account of his youth he could have no personal participation, it does not enter into the scope of this study to describe in detail the battles and internal struggles of the Italians in the cause of national unity. It will therefore only be expedient to briefly enumerate the principal stages of the great enterprize which triumphantly transported the throne of his father, King of United

Italy, to Florence, and eventually to that final goal so ardently desired—Rome.

The campaign of 1859 despite the glorious memories of Palestro, Magenta and Solferino, was nevertheless a deception to Victor Emmanuel and Cavour. The negotiations of Villafranca and Zürich were far from realizing the sanguine expectations Italy had based on the French intervention, while the cession of Nice and Savoy (1860) might justly be considered to have absolved the Italians from any sense of obligation toward their allies.

Count Cavour, who had felt constrained to tender his resignation on the conclusion of the campaign, and who had been succeeded by Rattazzi, was again at the head of the government in January, 1860. Owing to his indefatigable exertions and immense personal influence in March of the same year Emilia and Tuscany were, in consequence of an almost unanimous plebiscite, included in the monarchy.

Garibaldi's expedition to Sicily had been secretly encouraged and winked at by the government of Sardinia, which was prepared, however, in case of foreign complications arising therefrom, to officially disavow the

general's actions. In consequence of the
phenomenal success of the undertaking, and
the **decisive victory** of Volturno, together
with the flight of the Neapolitan Bourbons,
the minister **now** urged **Victor Emmanuel** to
risk an open **intervention in the** south before
matters **should** become entangled **by the intercession or** pretensions of foreign **diplomacy. In** order **to** adhere strictly to **the**
constitutional policy of the sovereign the
Chambers were convened **and asked to** sanction **the** admission **into the Kingdom of such
provinces of central and** southern Italy **as
should by popular vote manifest the desire.
Not only was the step sanctioned by the
Chambers, but a vote of** admiration and **national gratitude to Garibaldi, and his** brave
followers, was carried October 11, 1860.

The plebiscite in the Kingdom of the Two
Sicilies resulted, **as** was expected, in an overwhelming majority in favor **of annexation to**
the crown of **Savoy,** and **before his** death,
now close at hand, **Count Cavour** had the
satisfaction **of** seeing assembled at Turin **the**
first Italian Parliament, in which sat the **representatives** of twenty-one **million citizens.**

Even at this early stage it was recognized
that Rome must be the eventual capital of the

new Kingdom, and for the first time the world heard Cavour's utterance of his famous dictum "a free Church in a free State ; " for the great statesman then believed possible an accommodation with the Holy See.

On June 6, 1861, consternation spread over Italy with the news of the death, of typhoid fever, of Count Cavour.

The guiding hand had passed away, but the great impulse and noble ambitions which it had so wisely nurtured were strong enough now to stand alone. The "re galantuomo." the symbol of Honesty and Faith, round which almost all shades of political opinion could rally, did undoubtedly by his strong personality save his countrymen years of civil strife and the chaos of tentative forms of government, and it would be unfair to undervalue the influence of his subsequent magnificent labor, but it may safely be said that the genius of no one man was longer necessary for the inevitable ultimate success of Italian Unity.

Count Cavour's dying words were for Italy, and an expression of confidence in the great destinies awaiting his country. "It will go now," he muttered as the mists closed in darker, and the light of that magnificent intellect flickered and went out.

From 1859 to 1866 Venetia, still under Austrian rule, had followed wistfully the events in the other Italian states, eagerly awaiting the moment for her own liberation from the foreign yoke. The moment was full of promise. Austria and Germany having wrenched from Denmark the duchies of Schleswig-Holstein began to quarrel over the spoils, while Italy keenly watched the diplomatic controversy with a view to personal advantage from an open rupture between the two great Northern Powers.

In 1865 the Prussian Minister at Florence sounded the Italian Government concerning a combined attack on Austria, and, after protracted preliminaries, in April, 1866, a secret treaty of offensive and defensive alliance was concluded at Berlin. Among other clauses it was stipulated therein, that neither combatant was to grant an armistice, or effect a peace, until Austria had agreed to the cession of Venetia to Italy, and of **a** territory of equivalent population to Prussia. The treaty was to become null three months after the exchange of ratifications, if in the interval Prussia had not declared war on Austria.

The official notification of the opening of hostilities reached Florence on June **17**, 1866, and Italy immediately proceeded to fulfil her part of the contract by forwarding a declaration of war to the Archduke Albert, Commander-in-Chief of the Austrian forces in Italy.

Prince Amadeus was twenty-one years of age at the moment of the opening of the campaign of '66. He was now to receive that baptism of fire so eagerly sought by the princes of his House. That he had already had some practical experience of military affairs, in addition to the long years of patient and careful theoretical training, will be seen by the following statement of his services up to the date of the declaration of war against Austria.

The Prince received his first commission as Captain of the Fifth Infantry regiment under royal decree of March 14, 1859, when but in his fifteenth year. Sixteen months later he was promoted to be Major in the same regiment, and Lieutenant-Colonel of the same on June 1, 1861. In 1863 he is Colonel of Infantry, still inscribed on the rolls of the Aosta Brigade, and as such is, by royal decree of July 30, 1864, intrusted with the command of the First Infantry regiment at the Camp of Exercise of San Maurizio. Relieved of this command he is, on December 4, 1864, nominated Colonel of the Sixty-fifth Infantry regiment; in 1865 is transferred to the cavalry in command of the Novara Lancers, and finally, by decree of May 3, 1866, is Major-General commanding the Lombardy Grenadiers.

It is at the head of this brigade that we now find him going into action at Monte Croce.

General Brignone was in command of the division which included the Duke's brigade at Custoza. It being thought advisable to create a diversion on the enemy's flank, the General called up for this purpose the Lombardy Grenadiers, instructing Amadeus not to advance his brigade beyond certain limits until reinforcements had arrived. In the event of the movement proving unsuccessful the Prince was to withdraw his men to the well of Custoza, and there make a stand. In conformity with these orders Amadeus moved his brigade in the direction indicated, and soon found himself under fire. Shortly after Captain Cotti, an aide-de-camp, was killed at his side.

Followed by Major Balbo, Captain di San Marzano and Lieutenant Salvadego, his staff officers, the Prince now placed himself at the head of his brigade and led them in the assault of an Austrian battery which was causing great havoc amongst his men. In less than an hour the position was carried, the enemy's guns spiked, and the tri-color flag waving over the captured redoubt. The charge had been a gallant and brilliant one, but the cost of life was enormous.

As the Duke reined in his horse to survey the conquered position he afforded a target for the rifle of an Austrian sharp-shooter who lay in ambush, and whose bullet penetrated his chest.

A petty officer of his brigade, Alfonso Gibelli by name, was the first to reach his fallen chief, who made light of his wound, assuring those who crowded about him that it was a mere scratch. Aid having been procured, the Duke was placed on a mule and taken to the rear.

It is related that meeting a wounded soldier by the way, Amadeus insisted that he also be placed on the mule, and that, his comrade having fainted from loss of blood, the Duke held him in his arms during the entire painful journey, and on reaching the ambulance ordered the doctors to give their first care to the man's more serious wounds.

Amadeus passed the days of his convalescence at Monza, near Milan, where he was received by the populace with demonstrations of sympathy and affection.

His brilliant action brought the Prince the coveted medal **for** military valor, awarded only to **those who** have distinguished themselves on the field. **He** was also the recipient of an enthusiastically worded address in which the Municipality of Turin did homage **to** the " hero of Montecroce."

The valor of leaders **or men did not, however, maintain** the advantages **of the first engagements, and** Custoza **proved a lamentable defeat for the Italian flag.**

Although Turin had been superseded by Florence in its short-lived dignity **as capital** of the Kingdom of Italy, the **city by the Po** nevertheless retained **much of its social brilliancy, and** continued to be the headquarters **of** those members of **the Piedmontese** nobility whose official duties did not **require a** change of residence with **the** government. During **the** winter months the inmates of the lovely villas dotted over **the** surrounding country, and from the castles on the foot-hills **of the Alps,** flocked into the city, took possession **of** their huge palaces in the broad, windy streets, and defied the dreary snow-laden season with a never-ending series of gayeties.

Amadeus returned to Turin to complete his convalescence and was soon fully launched on the tide of pleasure. Young, good-looking and anxious to please, bringing with him, moreover, the glamour of brave deeds accomplished, the Prince rapidly became the most popular member of the brilliant throng in which he moved. The Italian is no snob; and although a royal prince is a personage the world over, in Italy to an extent infinitely less than elsewhere will birth give social popularity—or its semblance. As was to be expected the young Prince was received with every show of consideration and respect, but in addition to this his frank, manly dignity and genuine cordiality, mingled with a thoroughly democratic independence of character, rapidly endeared him to all with whom he was brought in contact.

It was not long before the social world of Turin became aware of the Prince's growing attentions to one of the most charming and beautiful young women of the aristocracy, the Princess Maria Victoria del Pozzo della Cisterna, at that time not quite twenty years of age. Her father, the Prince della Cisterna, belonged to one of the oldest noble houses of Piedmont, and through her mother, née Countess de Merode, the young Princess claimed relationship with the most distinguished families of the French and Belgian nobility.

The Prince's affections were visibly very seriously engaged, and naturally enough the affair gave rise to endless gossip and discussion, not entirely free from petty jealousy and malice. The majority held that it could only amount to a flirtation, as a member of the royal family would not be permitted to consult his personal inclination in a matter of such grave and far-reaching importance, and that political considerations would necessitate his seeking an alliance with the daughter of some Royal House. A mother's desire to safe-guard her daughter's peace of mind, as well as to free her house from the certain imputation of exaggerated ambition and low intrigue, decided the Princess della Cisterna to discourage the Duke's visits, and in consequence these were for a time discontinued, to the infinite chagrin of the parties most interested.

There were not lacking charmers who sought to console the unfortunate lover, but

4

their blandishments were lost on a nature one of whose chief characteristics was that of being thoroughly in earnest in all he undertook.

The Duke, sincerely in love, was in despair.

In his trouble he turned to a mutual friend, Signor Francesco Cassinis, President of the Chamber of Deputies, and besought him to plead his cause with the King.

Victor Emmanuel listened in silence to the Duke's ambassador. Finally he interrupted the eloquent flow of language by quietly asking: " Do the young people love each other?" " They idolize one another," replied the President. The King mused awhile, and then gruffly remarked: " Very well: they shall be married. It is not for me to stand in opposition to the sentiments of my sons."

The news of the King's consent to this alliance with a family not of royal blood caused considerable surprise, but the majority of Italians were pleased that the Prince should have selected a bride from amongst his own people, and cared not a jot if the rulers of minute German Principalities with marriageable daughters raised their eyebrows and sighed.

The preliminaries once arranged there was no reason for delay **and** preparations for the marriage were rapidly pushed forward.

The nuptials were celebrated at Turin **on** the 30th of May, 1867, amidst great pomp **and** splendor, the festivities and rejoicings being shared by patrician and populace alike. From all parts of Italy came congratulations **and** expressions of good will, while the municipalities of the larger cities sent splendid gifts and brilliant deputations.

A sad accident cast a gloom over the general light-heartedness, bringing mourning to many participating in the festivities. **Young Count Castigliole, a** dashing **cavalry** officer belonging **to** one **of the** most distinguished Piedmontese **families,** and an intimate personal **friend of the newly-married** couple, **was thrown from his horse while** riding in the pageant at the door of the royal carriage, and instantly killed. This shocking accident occurring at such **a** moment made **a** deep impression on the young Princess, who is said never to have forgotten the tragic scene.

On the termination of the campaign **of** 1866 Amadeus **had, in** accordance with the wishes **of** his father, begun to occupy him**self with** matters pertaining **to** the royal marine. After his marriage the Prince devoted himself exclusively to the study of naval science, receiving his commission as Vice Admiral on the Naval Staff in 1868. Before the close of this same year he was appointed Inspector General of the Royal Marine.

Within a year after his own marriage Amadeus was called upon to take a prominent part in the celebrations attending the wedding of his brother Humbert with his cousin the Princess Margaret of Savoy, daughter of the King's brother the late Duke of Genoa. The marriage, like that of Amadeus, was exceedingly popular in Italy, for the elder brother also cast in his lot with a princess of his own nationality. Besides, Italians cherished the memory of the bride's father, who had fought for national independence in 1848 and 1849, and had acquired a reputation for personal bravery and disinterested patriotism.

This wedding took place in Turin also, in the presence of the King, and brought together the various members of the royal family. From Paris came the bridegroom's sister the Princess Clotilde, by marriage a cousin of the Emperor of the French, while from Lisbon came his younger sister, Queen

Maria Pia of Portugal, for many years considered the best-dressed woman in Europe. The ill-fated Emperor Frederick, then Crown Prince of Prussia, also attended the wedding, and there first sowed the seeds of the cordial personal ties which continued unbroken to the hour of his death.

The public festivities on this occasion were among the most magnificent ever witnessed in Italy: more especially the great historical tournaments which took place in Turin and in the beautiful Cascine of Florence, presided over both in organization and execution by Prince Amadeus. Twenty-five years later (1893) a similar tournament took place in the Borghese gardens at Rome to celebrate the silver wedding of the King and Queen of Italy, in which participated their son the Crown Prince, and the three sons of Amadeus—the Duke of Aosta, Count of Turin, and Duke of the Abruzzi—while amongst the spectators sat the Emperor of Germany, the Empress, and a host of royal personages, come together to do homage to Italy's gracious sovereigns.

Victor Emmanuel took advantage of the general rejoicings on the occasion of his son's marriage to found the new order of the

Crown of Italy, which was created principally to honor those patriots who had contributed by their efforts and sacrifices to the shaping of the new and happy destinies of the Nation.

With the exception of the journeys necessitated by his official duties in connection with the navy the Duke continued to reside quietly in Turin, or with the Court at Florence, for many months after his marriage. On May 13, 1869, at Turin, a son was born to the royal couple. The boy was christened Emmanuel Philibert, and received from his grandfather the title of Duke of the Puglie, which he continued to bear until the death of his father in 1890, when he became Duke of Aosta in his turn.

But a few months after the birth of their son the Duke and Duchess started for Egypt, on board the "Castelfidardo," as the official representatives of the King of Italy at the splendid fêtes with which the Khedive, Ismail Pasha, inaugurated the opening of the Suez Canal. The "Castelfidardo" was accompanied by the national squadron as an escort of honor. During this expedition the royal pair visited the Holy Land, and while in Jerusalem the Duchess presented to the church

of the Holy Sepulchre all her private jewels,
amounting in value to over half **a million of
franes**.

On the return voyage an accident occurred
which endangered the safety of the steamer,
and the **lives of all** those on board. By the
bursting **of** one of **the** boilers several of the
crew were killed **and** many wounded. For
a time officers and men were panic-stricken.
Amadeus alone retained his presence of mind,
and by his calm and intelligent counsels succeeded in restoring confidence and **discipline ;**
personally lending **aid to the sufferers, and**
giving directions for temporary repairs. The
news of the **disaster,** together **with the admirable coolness** and aptitude displayed **by the
Prince, rapidly** spread over all Italy. Public
opinion advocated that the direction **of the**
navy, morally prostrated by the battle **of Lissa**
and distracted by **the dissensions of the various commanders,** should be given **to His Royal
Highness.** The suggestion was received with
special enthusiasm by sailors of all ranks, who
fully appreciated the fact that their **service**
could but gain by being placed under **so en-
lightened a** command, and who were moreover flattered that their **leader** should be one
standing so near the throne.

The naval manœuvres held that year under the Prince's direction were most successfully carried out, and strengthened the conviction that the young navy, under this fostering guidance, would rapidly become an efficient arm for the protection and development of the new Kingdom.

CHAPTER IV.

FOUR days previous to the declaration of war against Prussia by Napoleon III. (July 16, 1870), General Lanza received from the Marquis Visconti-Venosta a communication stating that the British Minister, on visiting him the day before, had read a telegram from Lord Granville announcing that the Spanish Government was prepared to do all in its power to nullify the Hohenzollern candidature for the throne, if it could rely on the acceptance of the Spanish Crown by an Italian prince. "As there is no time to lose," adds the Minister for Foreign Affairs, "I am starting for Leghorn to ascertain the views of the

Duke of Aosta, without in any way, however, compromising this government."

It was too late, however, for any substitution of the candidate to have averted the inevitable duel between the two great Powers which made the attempt to fill the vacant Spanish throne a pretext for a call to arms. It is now clear that the French Emperor, while fully realizing the peril his dynasty ran, was placed as it were between the Scylla of a foreign war, the issue of which was at best terribly doubtful, and the Charybdis of almost certain revolution at home, should he accept passively the supposed insult put upon his country. It is doubtful also whether the Iron Statesman beyond the Rhine would have been willing to let slip the opportunity to boldly stake on the fortunes of war the realization of his life's dream of a united Imperial Germany.

In 1868 the fall of the Spanish Bourbons and the flight of Queen Isabella from St. Sebastian to Pau left Spain a prey to revolution and party strife. From Santander to Malaga, from Cape Finisterre to the Gulf of Lyons, republicans, progressists, Carlists and royalists were at work issuing " pronunciamientos," framing or destroying constitutions, promising universal suffrage, liberty of the press, abolition of monopolies **and privileges**; or occupied in shooting down those **of their** countrymen whose political **views differed** from their own.

The provisional government **at** Madrid, which had assumed supreme **authority** under Marshal Serrano since the previous October, resigned its powers on February **22, 1869, to** the Cortes elected by universal suffrage, and without any serious disturbances. This body, however, confirmed **Serrano as chief of the** executive, and on **the 18th of the following** June nominated him Regent. **A few weeks later Marshal Prim announced to the Chamber the formation of the new** ministry, **of which he assumed the presidency.** Had **the election of a constituent assembly been undertaken immediately after the events in** Cadiz in **September, 1868, by which Queen** Isabella lost her throne, **it is** certain that little difficulty would then have been experienced in eliminating **the** republican **element** as a factor in national politics. The considerable delay which elapsed before **an** appeal to the nation was made, **and** the squabbles of the monarchists who, although unanimous **as** to principle, were totally in discord as **to** the

person of the sovereign, allowed socialist
agitators a fair field to secure a hold over the
masses and to instill the conviction that a
republican form of government was the only
one under which they could hope for peace
and justice.

The government at Madrid, convinced that
the monarchical system alone offered serious
guarantees of stability, which views were
equally shared by a large majority of the
members of the constituent Cortes, at once
began to cast about for a successor to the
throne.

After fruitless negotiations with Dom Ferdinand of Portugal, in conjunction with the
Utopian phantasm of an Hispano-Portuguese
Realm, attention was turned to Prince
Thomas, Duke of Genoa, as a candidate
likely to prove generally acceptable to Spaniards, belonging as he did to one of the most
liberal dynasties of Europe. In spite of the
Prince's being under age, and the consequent
necessity of a regency, a large portion of the
deputies viewed the selection with satisfaction. Prim even went so far as to consider
the fact of the Prince's being a minor as a
point in his favor, as it would permit of his
being instructed during the regency concern-

ing the political condition and wants of the country he was to govern. The project was, however, **soon** abandoned owing to the very decided opposition **of** the young duke's mother.

In the autumn **of 1868** negotiations were also attempted with Amadeus. The Prince being **at** that time Heir Presumptive to the Crown of Italy the proposals could not then **be** entertained.

Espartero, Duke della Vittoria, **who** had been appointed Regent of **Spain** during the **minority of Isabella, was the choice of a considerable faction in** the **Cortes. The old** soldier, **however,** positively refused **to allow** himself to be brought forward as a candidate, **both on account** of his **great age and the fact** that **he** possessed no heir. The **Duke of** Montpensier, a member of the Orleans family, was, by virtue of his marriage **with** the **sister** of the ex-Queen, a candidate whose popularity was more than doubtful. The name of Prince Leopold of Hohenzollern Sigmaringen had been brought forward **and** discussed, but abandoned on signs of evident dissatisfaction in France. Some **action on** the part of the government became **daily** more necessary. Prim, in reply **to an** interrogation in the

Chamber on May 7, 1870, expressed the universal desire to terminate the actual provisional political system, and frankly disclaiming any personal ambition, promised that the question should speedily be brought under consideration.

The Cortes were adjourned in June, 1870, until the following October, after having definitely voted the laws under discussion, and authorized the government to grant an amnesty whenever it should be judged opportune. A few days later the news arrived of the abdication of Queen Isabella in favor of her son the Prince of the Asturias, afterwards Alfonso XII., King of Spain. This document, signed on June 25, 1870, in the Basilewki palace in Paris, in the presence of the royal family and the more notable of the exiles who had followed the Court, hastened the solution of the existing crisis. In Madrid the problem of securing an acceptable successor to the throne became of the most acute interest, and it was evident a decision must be arrived at with the least possible delay. The Council of Ministers held on July 2, after mature deliberation, finally decided to officially notify the Powers that the national choice had fallen on the Prince of

Hohenzollern. On the seventh of the same month the Prince signified his acceptance of the Crown, provided his candidature be voted by the **Cortes.**

The news of the Prince's acceptance of the Spanish throne gave rise to the wildest tumult **in** Paris, where it was supposed to be **the result of an** intrigue **between** Prussia and the Spanish Marshal. French passions were thoroughly aroused in spite of the **em-phatic** denial of the Spanish government that the proposal had been planned in a **spirit** hostile to **France, or** that the negotiations **with Prince Leopold had passed** through **Count Bismarck's** hands, with **a view of** obtaining through his **influence the consent of** the King of Prussia.

The revocation by the Prince **of his former** acceptance, which was commun**icated to the** Powers on July **12,** might reasonably **have** been considered as putting **an end to** the controversy: but it was not so. The episode **in the** Ems Kurgarten, when **M.** Benedetti publicly accosted the King **of** Prussia and presented the latest demand **of** his government, gave Count Bismarck his opportunity. Next **day** the Berlin papers contained the following paragraph:

"When the intelligence of the hereditary Prince of Hohenzollern's renunciation was communicated by the Spanish to the French Government, the French Ambassador demanded of His Majesty the King, at Ems, that the latter should authorize him to telegraph to Paris that His Majesty would pledge himself for all time to come never again to give his consent, should the Hohenzollerns revert to their candidature. Upon this His Majesty refused to receive the French Ambassador again, and sent the aide-de-camp in attendance to inform him that His Majesty had nothing further to communicate to His Excellency."

Two days later a declaration of war was forced from the reluctant Emperor by his ministers and the maddened Parisian mob, and the fiercest struggle of modern times had begun.

The isolation of France in her hour of need was bitterly felt, and urgent appeals were made to Italy to join her old ally in the field; but although personally Victor Emmanuel would undoubtedly have desired to give aid, political obligations forbade his interference. Rome, and Rome alone, was the price demanded for any deviation from the line of strict neutrality ; and **Rome** the unhappy Emperor dared not **yield.**

Sedan, and the fall of the Empire, **gave** Italy **her long** awaited opportunity. On September 20, 1870, the King's troops marched through the Porta Pia amidst the enthusiastic acclamations of the Roman population. The last link in the **chain of** Italian unification was forged : **Rome became** the capital.

On the renunciation **of** the Prince of **Hohenzollern**, further attempts on **the** part **of** Spain to procure a King **were for a season postponed.** After **the** disaster **of Sedan, and the September revolution in** Paris, **the Madrid government** again initiated negotiations with **a view of obtaining from the House of Savoy a prince capable of guiding the helm on the** troubled sea **of Spanish politics.** The dynastic objections which **existed in 1868 in** regard to the acceptance **of** Prince Amadeus were no longer valid. **The birth of** the Prince of Naples in 1869 had provided Italy with an heir. **Marshal** Prim's propositions were consequently favorably received at Florence by the King, in spite **of the** Mexican catastrophe and cruel **fate of** Maximilian, still **so fresh in the** minds of all. Consent **to the Spanish request was** signified **on the**

condition that the Duke of Aosta be called
to the throne by a plurality of votes in the
Cortes, and that in order to obviate international complications, the good will of the
powers be obtained. In consequence a circular was issued from Madrid to the representatives accredited to the foreign Courts, noti-
fying them of the selection of the Duke as
the government's candidate for presentation
to the Cortes, and requesting the opinion of
the several sovereigns and cabinets on such
proceeding. Great Britain, Belgium, Portugal, France, Scandinavia, the North German
Confederation, Holland, Austria and Turkey
replied in favorable and friendly terms, while
Russia, in conformity with tradition, abstained
from any expression of opinion.

It had been no easy matter to persuade
the Prince to accept the candidature. He
honestly believed himself, or any alien, un-
equal to the task of restoring order or harmony among the factions at war in Spain,
and when he yielded it was in deference to
the wishes of others, and sorely against personal inclination and the dictates of his own
sound judgment. Perhaps he realized the
truth of the warning words of that experienced old monarch Louis Philippe in reference

to the urged intervention of France in the
Spanish affairs of 1835: " Let us help **the**
Spaniards from without, but don't let us get
into their boat ourselves. . . . **I** know them
well, they **are** ungovernable and not **to be**
tamed **by** strangers; they call us **in** to-day,
but **no** sooner there than they would detest
us, and would hinder us with all the means in
their power."

It is related that General Lanza, who had
been sent **to** secure the Duke's adhesion,
finding him stubborn in his refusal, **and** hav-
ing exhausted **all his** arguments **in vain,**
finally **remarked: "Your** Highness, **every
time** that **the interests of the State, or those
of Europe, have had need** of the **aid of a
Prince of the House of Savoy, such** aid has
never been refused. Would Your Highness
wish to be the first to act differently?"

The **words** made **an** impression on the
Prince, and his resistance was weakened
although not conquered.

" Come to-morrow," he replied, "and I will
give you an answer."

On the morrow the reply was in the affirm-
ative, but shortly after the Prince, moved
by some secret and irresistible impulse, again
wavered. Victor Emmanuel, who greatly de-

sired the realization of the project, but who refrained from the exercise of undue pressure on his son, conceived the plan of securing the Prince's acceptance by means of the influence of several officers of his household in whom special confidence was reposed. But this method met with signal failure.

The King—a keen observer, and also well aware of the generous and brave instincts of his son finally hit upon a little subterfuge which successfully overcame the Prince's reluctance.

"Of course," he remarked on an occasion when the topic was under discussion, "it is very hot in Spain at this time, and by going there you would also run the risk of a disagreeable adventure; perhaps even get a bit of lead in your ribs."

The idea that his refusal might be attributed to fear of bodily hurt was intolerable. There was danger to be affronted, and a service to be rendered to a people who, he was led to believe, saw in him the saviour of their political future. The sense of physical fear was unknown to the Prince; once persuaded of the rectitude of his action the possible risks he might run would merely add zest to the undertaking.

On this head many anecdotes are related,
and his contempt of danger exemplified.
One especially gives evidence of what might
almost be termed temerity. **The** day after
the dastardly attempt **on** his life in the via
Alcalà in Madrid, His Majesty started, **as**
had been **previously** arranged, on **a** tour **of**
the northern provinces. **On** his arrival at
St. Sebastian the police reported that **a con-**
spiracy was on foot to assassinate the sovereign, and that **the** assassins were probably at
that time in the town. **The King** listened
calmly to the report and warning, and shortly
after **retired for** the night. Next morning
consternation spread through the **palace when**
it became known **that on entering the bed-**
room at the usual hour the valet had found
no trace of his royal master. The palace and
town were scoured, and finally **His** Majesty
was discovered in the market-place sitting **on**
a barrel, with legs dangling, gossiping **in**
broken Spanish and chaffing the market
women, all of whom were perfectly aware of
the identity of their entertaining visitor.

On one of his pedestrian expeditions about
the streets of Madrid Amadeus met Signor
Castelar, then a rabid republican deputy, who,

to his no small astonishment, raised his hat in salute.

"What!" exclaimed the King. "Do you now uncover to royalty?"

"Not to royalty, Sire," was the quick reply, "but to the bravest man in Europe."

After all, Amadeus was told, he could hardly be considered a rank outsider, and even rabid nationalists might be brought to acknowledge his right to cast in his lot with theirs. The House of Savoy had a title of reversion on the Crown of Spain. Philip V., by a royal decree which formed an integral part of the treaty of Utrecht, had declared on November 5, 1712, that by failure of his legitimate descendants he should be succeeded by the Duke of Savoy, and by failure of the male line, by Prince Amadeus of Carignano and his sons, who, as descendants of the Infanta Catherine, daughter of Philip II., had a clear and recognized right to the throne of Spain.

The acceptance of the Prince once obtained, the Madrid government, at the opening of the Cortes, on November 3, 1870, formally presented Amadeus of Savoy, Duke of Aosta, as a candidate for the throne.

Marshal Prim, after having exposed the honorable motives which prompted the withdrawal of the Prince of Hohenzollern, expatiated at length on the titles possessed by the new candidate to win the love and admiration of Spaniards of every political shade. The announcement was received with expressions of varied significance by the republican, legitimist and Montpensier factions.

On November sixteenth, the date fixed for the discussion **and vote,** the Cortes was crowded, and from the outset it was evident the session would be **a** stormy one. Proceedings opened at half-past **two,** under the presidency of Don Manuel Ruiz-Zorrilla, with the reading **of** letters from three deputies prevented by illness from attending the session. **One desired his vote should be recorded for the Duke of Aosta ; the second declared** himself in favor of Espartero, while **the third** cast his ballot for the Duke of Montpensier. Later the protests of Spaniards adverse to the candidature of the Italian prince were taken note of, and gave rise to an outbreak **of** wild tumult and disorder, during which mutual recriminations and accusations of disloyalty were hurled against the various **leaders.** During **the** tempest the names of **those who,** having been fervent partisans of Isabella, had with equal fervor proclaimed her fall, were read to the Assembly, and promptly seized upon to sneeringly estimate the value of a certain loyalty which the future monarch could count upon. A barrier was finally opposed to the torrent of abuse and vituperation by the energy of the President who opportunely unearthed a law by virtue of which at the election of a monarch all discussion was prohibited during the eight days preceding such election, and by force of which consequently no protests could either be read or listened to.

Order having with difficulty been re-established, the voting was finally proceeded with by means of tickets on which each member wrote the name of his candidate. Three hundred and eleven members took part in the ballot—the number of deputies entitled to vote being three hundred and forty-five. The result gave the Duke of Aosta one hundred and ninety-one votes in the Chamber, plus two votes given by deputies who were absent. The majority required by the law for the election of a monarch was one hundred and seventy-three. Espartero obtained but eight votes. Prince Alfonso, son of Isabella II., received two. Sixty-three members voted for the republic in one form or another. The

Duke of Montpensier **counted** twenty-seven voices in his favor, while his wife, the sister of the ex-queen, received, but a single one. Nineteen blank tickets were cast, twelve **of** which were returned by Carlist members.

The secretary **of** the Cortes having read the result, **Don** Manuel Ruiz-Zorrilla solemnly announced that the Duke of Aosta had been legally elected King of Spain.

Colonel Garcia Cabrera at once started for Italy, the bearer of a letter from Marshal Prim to Victor Emmanuel, informing His Majesty **of the result of** the election, **and** giving the assurance that the great majority of the **people, as well** as the army and navy, enthusiastically applauded **the** selection. Shortly afterwards the official deputation, **appointed** by the Cortes to solemnly tender the crown to Prince Amadeus, left Madrid with President Ruiz-Zorrilla at its head. At Cartagena the envoys embarked on **the** vessels of a squadron held in readiness, and set sail for Genoa. The latter port enforced a quarantine of several days, duration on the deputation, **as** yellow fever had broken out at Barcelona, and it was feared that Cartagena was also infected.

In the meanwhile preparations were rapidly

pushed forward in Florence for the solemn reception of the envoys.

"What a delightful task it would be for some modern Pepys to describe the festivities we are now witnessing here in honor of the Spanish Deputation sent to offer the throne of Ferdinand and Isabella to Amadeo di Savoia." Thus exclaims one of the numerous correspondents from the Florence of December, 1870.

And indeed the glitter of official gold lace and the flash of brilliant-studded orders—the rushing to and fro of court equipages, and the magnificence of the Spanish accessories, kept the good Florentine burghers open-mouthed with admiration. Fifty-five members composed the delegation, and the government was sorely perplexed as to where to lodge the principals and suites of this gorgeous host. Finally it was decided to house them at a public hostelry, the Albergo della Città, as none of the government or municipal palaces were available, while Prince Corsini graciously tendered his beautiful palace, hard by on the Lung' Arno, for banquets and soirées.

International opinion as to the wisdom of Amadeus in accepting the Spanish Crown, and as to the possibility of his mantaining the same, differed very widely and ranged from the absurdly optimistic to the darkest depths of pessimism.

In the light of subsequent events it is curious to revert to a leader which appeared in the London " Times " of November 19, 1870.

" We do not share the opinion of those who look upon the position accepted by the Italian Prince as 'anything but a bed of roses.' The strongest objection that the grandiloquent Castelar was able to urge against Amadeus was his alien nationality— a circumstance which, after all, only exposes Spain to such a humiliation as England and Belgium and France, and almost all the noblest and freest nations in the world. Spain herself not excepted, cheerfully submitted to at some time or other. Against the Prince personally, even inexorable Republicanism had nothing to say . . . that Prince Amadeus and his Duchess are, by their personal qualities, calculated to win the good will of the sound part of the Spanish nation is a point on which no doubt need be entertained. The Duke has sense and courage, tact, discretion, and that happy mixture of dignity and winning affability which covered a multitude of his father and his grandfather's sins. He is twenty-five years old, a married man with children, and his heir bears the name of Emmanuel Philibert—the name of that Prince of Savoy to whose genius Spain is indebted for the most signal victory her arms ever obtained over those of France.* Both the duke and his consort—the last born a subject, though of noble rank—have been the most popular members of the royal family in Italy, and especially at Naples, where the House of Savoy was till lately as utter a stranger as it was in Spain, and where it had long been the object of inveterate prejudice."

On December 4th, Victor Emmanuel received the Delegation in solemn audience in the throne-room at the Pitti Palace, and with all the pomp and ceremony befitting the important mission on which it came. The delegates were conveyed to the palace in carriages of state, and received by the sovereign, Amadeus at his right, surrounded by the Princes, Ministers and great dignitaries of the Kingdom. The Spanish Envoy having officially presented the Deputation, Señor

* Emmanuel Philibert, " Tête de Fer." Battle of Saint Quentin, 1557.

Ruiz-Zorrilla **gave** utterance **to the** following:

"Sire : **We** come as representatives of the Constituent Cortes to offer to your son, His **Royal** Highness the Duke of Aosta, the crown **of** Spain, and Your Majesty being the head **of** the family of the illustrious Prince, it **is of** you that we respectfully crave permission to do so. Before Your Majesty grants the permission we hope for, it must **be** permitted **us to** express our profound gratitude for **the** honors and courtesies which have been lavished upon **us from the** moment we reached **the shores of** Italy. Having **received these honors by** virtue of the mandate and the **representation** with which we are vested, **we shall take pleasure** in communicating these proofs of consideration and benevolence **to** the Constituent Cortes, as now, making ourselves its faithful interpreters, **we** offer prayers **to** Heaven for the prosperity of your Kingdom ; **for** the happiness and grandeur of Italy."

To which the King made reply : " By your request, gentlemen, you render a great honor to my dynasty and to Italy, and at the same time demand a sacrifice of my heart. I grant my consent to my beloved son's acceptance of the glorious throne to which the voice of the Spanish people calls him. I am convinced that, by the aid of Divine Providence, and the confidence of your noble Nation, he will be enabled to accomplish his high mission for the prosperity and for the grandeur of Spain."

Ruiz-Zorrilla then turned to the Duke, addressing him in the following words: "Most Serene Sir: The Constituent Cortes of the Spanish Nation, terminating the great and delicate mission entrusted it by the liberal suffrage of the people, in the solemn public session held on the sixteenth ultimo, elected Your Highness to the throne. By virtue of the honorable confidence reposed in us by the Cortes we come to acquaint Your Highness with the vote of the representatives of a People, master of its destinies, and to invite you to accept this spontaneous offer, placing on your brow this crown of Spain made famous by the glorious deeds of a hundred monarchs. This is not the place to examine into the causes of our recent political revolution, but we would recall to Your Highness that our national history at every page records loyalty to the monarch, fealty to the oath, and at the same time the affection and tenacity with which the Spanish people have always guarded their privileges and their liberties. The monarchical sentiment of the Spanish nation, rooted by the unbroken traditions of centuries in the hearts of the various social classes, and bound to-day in close alliance with the ideal of modern justice, exacts that the monarchy which represents our glories and fills our past, should be founded on national sovereignty, and should be perpetuated by the aid of all, strong in the indestructible legitimacy of its origin. Thus will it surely contribute to the prosperity and grandeur of our country—the aim of our endeavors, the constant object of our most cherished hopes. With a view to this great and glorious end the Spanish Cortes have sought in that House of Savoy, which, by its identification with the national sentiment of noble Italy, has shaped her prosperous destinies by the aid of liberal institutions, a Prince whom they may invest with the august dignity, and on whom they may confer the high prerogatives, attributed by the Constitution of 1869 to the Monarch. Spain hopes to find in Your Highness a King who, proclaimed by the love of the nation and solicitous of her weal, shall heal the wounds

opened in her heart by continual misfortune,
and which have weakened the might by which
in former days she prevailed, divining and fostering the genius of the Immortal Genovese
to conquer for civilization a new world, while
by her deeds she aroused the old to the appreciation of the splendor of her glory.   Nevertheless, the cradle of so many heroes is dead
neither to Future nor to Hope!   She was
decadent and prostrate when, at the opening
of this century, her King a prisoner, her territory invaded, she astonished the world by
the vigor, by the heroism with which she
fought, until she hurled the invader from her
soil and regained her lost independence.   A
people which still is capable of such virile
energy, and which inscribes in the Temple
of Immortality the names of its sons and its
cities, has the right to believe its misfortunes
transitory, and to trust that Providence will
compensate it for its sufferings by leading it
to new and higher destinies.   In the name
of the Spanish People, we, their representatives, offer you the Crown.   Our most honorable mission accomplished, it rests with
Your Highness to decide whether to rule the
destinies of Spain, whose ancient glories have
often been associated with those of your

family, and whose old Kings **are your** ancestors, offer a sufficient incentive to the lofty aspirations **of a** young prince desirous of emulating by his deeds the great examples **of** his predecessors."

Amadeus **was** deeply moved during the delivery **of** his reply : so deeply **at** times that his sentences became almost inaudible to those nearest him, and it was apparent to **all** that the tremendous responsibilities he was about to assume weighed heavily on the conscientious prince. No doubt the probable ultimate consequence **of** the step was clearly before his mind. As we have **said** Victor Emmanuel had set his heart on **the** acceptance **of** this brilliant offer which he rightly called an **honor to** his dynasty and to Italy, and which **might** be construed **as** a glorious recognition **of** the policy **of** straightforward honesty so persistently pursued since **the** accession to the throne of " il re galantuomo." Nevertheless the analogies between his son's future position and that of Maximilian must have thrust themselves on his mind, and even the repeated and optimistic assurances of the over-sanguine Prim **can** hardly have allayed all apprehension. **It is** more probable that the old fearlessness of Casa Savoia—that

6

contempt of danger in any shape or form—
and the strict, unquestioning sense of duty,
prompted the desire to see his son undertake
the noble task. When after Custoza Victor
Emmanuel was informed of the wound which
had laid Amadeus low, and of Humbert's
peril during the charge of Austrian cavalry,
it was the soldier's voice which spoke before
that of the father: " Dead or wounded, what
matters it so long as my sons are not prisoners." Followed shortly by an outburst of
paternal enthusiasm : " Blood does not lie !
Bravo Amadeus ! "

The manly modesty and frank opinions expressed in the Prince's reply convinced all
who heard him of the sincerity of his emotion,
and of the earnestness with which he undertook the duties thrust upon him.

" Gentlemen," he began ; " the eloquent
speech of your Honorable President has increased the natural and profound agitation
which the vote of the Constituent Assembly
of Spain had already caused me. With a
heart full of gratitude I will briefly set before
you the reasons which have prompted my accepting, as I do here before you accept with
the aid of God and with the consent of the
King my father, the ancient and glorious

crown you come to offer me. God had
already granted **me an** enviable destiny
Born of an illustrious dynasty, participating
in the glories and fortunes of my ancient
House without having the responsibilities **of**
government, I had before me a pleasant and
happy existence, during which occasions
have not failed in the past nor would be likely
to be lacking in the future, of usefully serving my country. **You** have come, Honorable
Sirs, to open to me a far larger horizon. **You**
call me to fulfil obligations, great **at any**
time, but more than ever formidable in these
**times of ours. Faithful to the traditions of
my** ancestors, who never **swerved either before a duty or in the face of peril,** I accept
the noble and lofty mission which Spain **con-
fides to me,** although **I am** not unaware **of the**
difficulties of my new task, nor of the responsibility I assume before **History. But I trust**
in God who sees the rectitude **of** my intentions, and I place confidence in the Spanish
People so justly proud of their independence,
of their great religious and political traditions,
and who have given proof of their ability to
combine with **order the** passionate and ungovernable **love of** liberty. Gentlemen: **I
am still too young** and the acts of my life are

too unworthy for me to attribute to personal
merit the choice which the Spanish Nation
has made. You have considered, I am sure,
that Providence has granted to my youth that
most fruitful and most useful education—the
spectacle of a people reconquering its independence through close union with its King,
and the faithful adherence to liberal institutions. You desire that your country on
which Nature has lavished all her gifts and
History all its glories, shall also enjoy this
happy unity which has made, and always will
continue, I trust, the prosperity of Italy.   It
is to the glory of my father, and the fortune
of my country, that I am indebted for my
election, and in order to render myself worthy
of it I can only loyally follow the example
of the constitutional traditions which have
guided my education.   A soldier in the army
I will be, Gentlemen, the first citizen before
the representatives of the nation.   The annals
of Spain are full of glorious names ; knightly
deeds ;   wonderful, great captains ;   navi-
gators ; famous Kings !   I know not whether
it will be granted me to shed my blood for
my new country, or if it will be vouchsafed
me to add a page to the many which illustrate
the glories of Spain.   But in any event I am

very certain, because this much depends **on**
myself and not **on my** destiny, that Spaniards
will always be able to say of the King of their
choice: 'His loyalty rises above party strife ;
he has nought in his heart beyond the desire
for concord and the prosperity of the Nation.'"

The **ceremony was** concluded by the reading of the formal deed of acceptance, which
was duly signed by the King-Elect, Victor
Emmanuel, the Marquis Visconti Venosta
and Señor Ruiz-Zorrilla.

Next day **Victor Emmanuel** notified the
Italian **Parliament of his son's accession to the**
Spanish **throne, and dwelt in terms of pride
and affection on the compliment** paid his dynasty, **while expressing** his confidence in the
ability **of the Prince to** faithfully guide **the**
sister **country in the path of Peace and Prosperity.**

CHAPTER V.

ON the conclusion of the ceremonies and fêtes at Florence attending his investiture of the high dignity conferred upon him, Amadeus returned to Turin to confer with the Duchess who, still suffering from the effects of her recent confinement (Count of Turin, born in Turin, November 24, 1870), had been unable to accompany her husband to the capital.

It was now arranged, the King's immediate presence being necessary at Madrid, that Maria Victoria with her two sons should follow when she had sufficiently regained her strength, while Amadeus set out alone for the country of his adoption.

After a hasty visit **to** Florence, where he **remained but a few hours** in order to receive his father's blessing and bid **a** final farewell to the other members of his family, Amadeus left on Christmas night for Spezia, there to embark on the Spanish frigate which was to convey him to Barcelona. The King-Elect was accompanied thus far on his journey by his brother Prince Humbert and Prince Eugene Carignano. General Cialdini, with the rank **of** special Ambassador **to** the King of Spain, was to escort his royal master as far as Madrid.

At noon **on December 26th, on the arrival** of the train at Spezia, the **royal party at once proceeded** to the harbor to embark on the " Numancia " which was lying **at anchor in the** bay. The weather was dull and dreary, and snow fell as the launch left the quay. Besides the local authorities and officials but **few** persons had ventured forth **to** witness the departure of the Prince. **A** feeble attempt at a cheer was made as the party left the landing-stage, but the proceedings were characterized throughout by moral as well as atmospheric depression, and even the Spanish officials showed but little enthusiasm **in spite of the thunder of the** guns, and brave display of bunting of the assembled war vessels.

As Prince Humbert and the other visitors left the " Numancia " Amadeus uttered the prophetic words: " I go to fulfil an impossible mission. Spain, now divided into various parties, will unite against a foreign King, and I shall soon be obliged to return the crown they have offered me."

To the reply that the well-known loyalty of the House of Savoy would disarm and conquer his enemies, he sadly murmured, " My loyalty will not be able to save me from the fury of the contending factions."

Doubtless the warning words of Mendez Vigo, uttered a few days previously, were in the Prince's mind. In a furious attack on the President of the Council, accusing him of manufacturing out of whole cloth the enthusiastic reports of the welcome which would be accorded the Duke of Aosta in Spain, Vigo, had exclaimed: " I am a loyal Spaniard, and I owe the truth to the King-Elect. I ask him before he enters Spanish territory to employ some means of ascertaining the true opinion of the Spanish people."

Meanwhile it must not be supposed that Queen Isabella calmly submitted without

protest to what she naturally considered the usurpation **of** the rights of her son Don Alfonso, in whose favor she had abdicated a throne she in truth no longer possessed. From Geneva a vigorously worded manifesto was launched :

" The revolution continues its career, **and** has **just** disavowed the rights of my son,—who is to-day your legitimate King according **to** all the Spanish Constitutions,—by calling to the throne of St. Ferdinand and of Charles V. a foreigner, whose merits, however **great,** cannot entitle him to be your Sovereign **in the face of the rights of a** whole dynasty, the **only one which has in** its favor **that** legiti- **macy,** consecrated **by the** lapse of ages and **by** constitutions **which** it has **been** a signal **folly** to disavow."

The ex-Queen then adds that she would not restore the throne to her son at the cost of Spanish blood, enough of which has been already shed, but that she enters this solemn protest, and is confident that when the rev- olutionary torrent has spent itself, the res- toration may be brought about pacifically.

Similar pronunciamentos from the pen of Don Carlos stimulated the energies of his partisans, who had proclaimed him King in the famous assembly held at Vevey, Switzerland, on April 18, 1870 ; on the conclusion of which the royal exile had actually constituted a ministry, and distributed military commands in the Peninsula to which he dared not himself return.

Political passions ran high in Madrid, while in the provinces the situation was further complicated by the efforts of the Alphonsists. Carlists, Republicans, and, last but not least, the members of the "Internacional." The prospects for a peaceful accession of the new Ruler were doubtful at best, when an event occurred which shook the political fabric to its foundations, and deprived the Crown at a blow of its chief support.

With the assassination of General Prim the possibility of the foundation of a foreign dynasty in Spain vanished. By virtue of the combined prestige of Prim and Serrano it might have floated a while longer than it did, but with the disappearance of either it must inevitably have sunk below the overwhelming blood of national opposition.

The session of the Cortes on December 27, had been marked by violent denunciation on the part of the opposition to the new régime. In vain had Prim argued, stormed and pleaded, surpassing himself in his effort to shield the sovereign whose advent he so impatiently awaited.

Laboring under great excitement, which he made no attempt to conceal, the General, in company with **two** of his aides-de-camp, **left the** Cortes after dark **to** drive to the Ministry of **War. As** the carriage entered **the** narrow Calle **del** Turco it was stopped **by a** party of armed men and the General **fired** upon at close range. The assault was so sudden and unexpected that no attempt could **be made** to seize the aggressors, who promptly took to flight. Nine shots had taken effect; **seven in the** left shoulder and **two in the** right hand. **Covered with blood the** General sank in the arms of **an** aide-de-camp, while the carriage was driven at full gallop to his residence. In spite of the gravity of the wounds and **the necessary** amputation **of** his fingers, the doctors did not at first apprehend a fatal termination. For two days Madrid hovered between hope and despair; on the third fever ensued, and **at** half-past eight o'clock on the evening of December 30, but a few hours before the arrival of the King on whose brow he had labored so persistently to place the crown, **Prim** expired.

The first news which greeted Amadeus when the "Numancia" cast anchor in the harbor of Carthagena, was that of the assassination of the man to whom he must naturally turn for guidance and advice on taking up the reins of government. Nor were the motives for the assassination obscure or far to seek. If Prim had found death at the hands of his political adversaries, yet countrymen withal, for the part he had played in attempting to bring peace to his distracted country, there could be but little doubt that the foreign Ruler, whose importation was so bitterly resented, would from the outset become the target of every discontented dagger within the realm.

Yet Amadeus hesitated not a moment. Turning to those around him he sadly exclaimed : "Gentlemen, my duty is clear. Let us get on to Madrid."

Passing the night at Aranjuez, where his reception by the populace was cold and forbidding, the King reached Madrid about noon on January 2, 1871.

An official reception had been prepared for the new King, and the approaches to the station, and streets through which he must pass, were thronged with vast crowds assembled, in spite **of the bitter** cold and snow, to witness the arrival **of** the sovereign. A state carriage was in waiting to convey him to the Cortes. Declining this the King signified his intention of entering the capital on horseback.

As the brilliant escort of generals and aides-de-camp started it soon became evident to Amadeus that special precautions were being devised by the members of his suite to surround him in such manner as to prevent any possible contact with the public crowd for fear of insult, or **worse.** The King thereupon requested all accompanying him to fall back, and rode alone several paces in advance of his brilliant following.

From the railway station the King proceeded direct to **the church of** Atocha where **the** remains of **Prim lay in state.** A large painting representing the scene hangs in the apartments **of the** Ducal Palace in Turin. The general lies in his unclosed coffin, in full uniform, his hands folded upon his breast. Four tall candles burn at the corners of the **low** platform on which the bier rests. Amadeus stands **beside** the corpse, his hands clasped upon his sword, his head bowed in grief. **At a** respectful distance hovers a brilliant group **of** generals, diplomatists and statesmen, while in the background a half-dozen priests recite the prayers for the dead.

What a contrast from the grim presence of death to the scene in the Cortes, where the young King now goes to take the oath and receive the homage of his new subjects!

As he glanced round the serried ranks of members of both branches of the Cortes, Amadeus knew that even here amongst those assembled to give him official greeting were inexorable foes, morally responsible if not directly accountable for the political crime which had deprived him of his staunchest ally. Not even the glittering uniforms of the representatives of army, navy and diplomacy, or the sumptuous toilettes of the Court Ladies, dazzling with jewels and gay with flowers, could efface the sombre memory of the silent form lying yonder in the church of the Atocha, and which should have been so conspicuous a figure near the throne. To the sensitive ears of the new King the enthusiastic and prolonged cries of welcome which greeted his entrance had a false ring, noticeable even under the emotion they caused.

On the entrance of the King, the President arose and read the following message from the Regent:

" Deputies: The revolution of 1868, initiated through the bravery of the army and navy, **and** prepared by national sentiment, has **become** personified in this Constituent Assembly which, comprehending the needs of the country, has given satisfaction to liberal aspirations while preserving peace and order, granting **a** fundamental code having as its basis democratic principles, guaranteed by **a** monarchy, the more lofty and worthy of respect emanating as it does from the popular sovereignty. The constitution having been **voted,** the Assembly desired **to develop the system** adopted by **it, and while the election of the Prince who was to occupy the throne was being** prepared, placed its confidence **in me, rendering me the high honor of entrusting** to me public **affairs and the direction of the** policy framed by **the Chamber.** I, from that moment **desirous** of accomplishing with loyal impartiality **the duty you** charged me with, have had, in common with the Chamber, the responsibility of the important interval which closes to-day. Nevertheless **I do** not regret traversing so many and such difficult trials since they have left us all the consciousness of **the** fulfilment **of** duties imposed upon us by **our country. The day has** at length arrived on which your labor is terminated, and on which I must resign the powers which, to enable me to assist you in accomplishing an end, you confided to me. With an easy conscience I abandon the high magistracy with which you invested me, hoping the verdict of my country will be benign, and considering myself rewarded with the opinion you have formed as to my conduct ; which opinion remains impressed on my most sacred feelings. May God grant the fervent prayers I offer up to Him for the prosperity and future of my dear country. May our fellow-citizens gratefully cherish the memory of this Assembly whose labors result in the monarchy we inaugurate to-day, and towards which we all look for the happiness of this noble nation."

Grand words, and modest, coming as they did from one in whose hands had so long lain the destiny of a great nation, and from one who, looking only to what he considered the public good, had so strenuously rejected all temptation for personal aggrandizement.

The constitution of 1869 having been read, His Majesty arose and took solemn oath to accept and defend the same, as well as the laws of the Kingdom. The President then turning to the chamber amidst enthusiastic applause proclaimed Amadeus **I.** King of Spain.

The Constituent Cortes, its labors having ended with the **election** and proclamation of the Sovereign, was now declared dissolved, and the responsibilities and cares of government devolved upon the young Monarch.

The first official act of the new Ruler consisted **in** the selection of a ministry, the **formation** of which was naturally enough entrusted to Marshal Serrano. The Marshal himself Prime Minister **and** Minister **of War,** gathered round him a composite cabinet into which entered **such** various **political ingredients of the liberal-monarchical factions as** Ruiz-Zorrilla, Martos **(Foreign** Affairs), **Ulloa,** Sagasta, Moret, **Ayala** and Beranger. **This ministry entered upon** its **official being** on January **4, 1871.**

On the 13th General **Cialdini was** received by the King with all the pomp and ceremony befitting his high mission, and delivered into His Majesty's hands **the** letter **of** Victor Emmanuel accrediting him **as** Ambassador Extraordinary **to** congratulate the new Sovereign on his accession. The general expressed to His Majesty the sorrow of the Italian people **at** losing a prince so greatly and deservedly

7

beloved, but gave utterance also to the wide-spread conviction that the Prince's origin could but strengthen the sympathies and interests of the two nations, already so closely related by ties of blood and racial affinities.

Towards the middle of February Queen Maria Victoria who, on account of her recent confinement had, as will be remembered, not been able to accompany her husband, set forth on her journey to join the King at Madrid. The effort proved, however, too great for her feeble condition, and by the time Alassio was reached a violent attack of fever obliged the royal patient to again take to her bed. The Queen's illness assumed so threatening an aspect that little hope of her recovery was entertained and the sacrament was administered. Victor Emmanuel and various members of the royal family hastened to the bedside of the invalid, but the exacting duties of his position kept the anxious husband far from the side of the wife he so tenderly loved, and this enforced absence was perhaps one of the bitterest trials of his brief career as King—so full of deception and disappointment.

Three weeks after her convalescence was fully established Her Majesty was enabled to continue her journey to Onelia, thence to em-

Maria Victoria, Queen of Spain

bark **on March** 8, only **to** be tossed by tempestuous seas **and** battered by a series of violent storms for ten mortal days until finally **the** frigate cast anchor off Alicante. Here **Amadeus met his consort** and escorted her with their two young sons to Madrid.

The absorbing interest which now occupied **the** public mind was the election of members **to** the Cortes which were to meet on April 3. **The** problems confronting the government were numerous and serious ones essentially demanding a fusion **of party and personal interests with those of the nation. For the readjustment of the greatly impaired finances the cessation of the** distracting **political conflicts** still **actively carried on in the** provinces **was** imperatively necessary. **Spain must** have peace within her borders. **The** restoration of harmonious relations **with the Holy** See was also greatly to be desired, without however the sacrifice of the ecclesiastical reforms obtained at such great cost, and which **placed the** country on a par with those nations professing amongst their liberal institutions freedom **of** worship and independence from the tyranny of the Church in matters **temporal.** If Spain **was to** take **her** place amongst the **great Powers of Europe as** a liberal and constitutional nation, governed according to the ideas of the times, anarchy and rebellion must be stamped out, and a fair field given to the representatives of the system of government chosen by her sons. The sequel of the revolution of September demonstrated that the Spanish people did not confound the monarchical principle with the causes which had produced the downfall of the late dynasty, and this fact was still further confirmed by the action of the Constituent Assembly and the object the Carlists, or rebels as they were called, had in view. The republican element was as yet a factor which, although it could not safely be overlooked, was, however, no serious menace to the established government; but the troublesome Carlist following, and the possibility of a fusion of one or several independent factions with this party, caused the ministry to anticipate the approaching elections with considerable apprehension.

The result proclaimed a not insignificant ministerial majority in both houses of Parliament, and the political atmosphere seemed less dangerously charged with brewing storm than had been anticipated when, on the date fixed, Amadeus opened the session with a speech impregnated with wise and conciliatory utterances. **Alas!** If the opening ceremonies were characterized by calm and apathy the brief lull **was all** too soon **to** be followed by violent controversy and bitter denunciation. The imperfectly appreciated republican strength vied with the relentless **animosity** of the Carlistos in every possible **endeavor** to thwart the projects and aims of the government to attain dignified stability and national prosperity. Patriotism was thrown to the winds in the **wild** attempt to harass the " foreigner " whose aid and counsel the country **had so recently invoked,** and **who was so** loyally struggling to **reconcile** the **rigor** necessary to **quell** illegal disorder **with the** chivalric interpretation of constitutionality characteristic **of his House.**

In 1871 the Spanish people, and **by people** should be understood **not merely the " plebs "** —rural and urban—but the nation in its component parts, **was little** prepared **to** comprehend or appreciate the advantages of a liberal government. Those in contact with the masses in the fields or the factory ; those in communion with the middle classes, as well as those influencing the opinions of the aristocracy, had in their hands a terrible weapon wherewith to damn the **King's** every endeavor. Was he not the son of the excommunicated despoiler of the High Priest of Christendom! Were they not aware that Pius IX. was a prisoner in his palace, his capital and his territory wrenched from him! This influence cannot be over-estimated in a study of the causes of Amadeus's failure. The opposition came from below as well as from those adherents to the old régime, and the more liberal the institutions granted, the more surely and quickly must the sap of political-religious intrigue rise through the heart and trunk of the Nation—its Assembly—until it permeated the topmost branches of the Administration.

Any one of the unsuccessful foreign candidates would have shared the same fate, and possibly in addition have plunged the country deep in bloodshed and civil strife before being compelled to yield. While this is undoubtedly true, it is no less a fact that the political events in Italy in 1870, and his connection with the authors of them, handicapped the Italian prince to an extent either little suspected, or under-estimated, at the time. Any ruler, foreign or native, brought to power by the leaders of the revolution of 1868 and the authors of the reforms which sprang therefrom, **would** have **been** held responsible by the reactionary and ultra conversative parties for the coldness existing with the Vatican, and would undoubtedly, sooner or later, have paid **the** penalty **of his** temerity by **being** forced either to abdicate or rescind the offensive measures. This being the case the Holy See could hardly be expected to view with complacency the possession of the throne of the most catholic monarchy in Europe **by** the son of the occupant of the Quirinal. The young prince was noted in **Italy for** his broad and liberal views; and at that moment neither **broad nor liberal views were looked** upon with favor in the **Vatican. The Liberal Pope of 1848** had **long since been** transformed **into a** prudent **and** wily diplomatist who carefully **avoided the edged tools** he had played with in his early years; and **the later** Pontiff who was to coquette with radicalism was then occupied in composing Latin verses in Perugia.

Evidences of the vacillation and bad faith of some **of** those **who** had been loudest and most persistent in their appeals for his acceptance of the crown were thus early thrust upon the young Sovereign. It soon became apparent that he must either allow himself to become a mere **tool** tossed **from the** grasp of one designing politician to another, to the detriment of the best interests of the nation whose institutions he had sworn to safeguard, or pass beyond the spirit, if not the letter, of the constitution he had taken oath to defend and uphold. It must be remembered that from the outset Amadeus fully recognized the eventuality of his abdication; but it would be to grossly misunderstand the fibre of the man to assume that he had not also determined to make at least a desperate struggle to assert and uphold the majesty of his office, and only to yield when every attempt at conciliation had failed, and he could clearly no longer combine royal dignity and self-respect with the fulfilment of his constitutional pledges.

In the opening pages of this study some idea of the events which marked the early years of the young prince's life has been given, and the writer has endeavored to lay stress on the immense influence of these in the formation of the character of Amadeus. From tenderest infancy he had witnessed the varying fortunes of the struggle for independence and unity in the land of his birth. He had assisted at the national or parliamentary checks, or advantages, which marked the progressive policy of his father and the great ministers who served him. Defeat and disappointment were no strangers to him ; despair and humiliation had visited his House. But he had had instilled into his very nature that reverence for the constitutional rights of the people which had in the end carried his father triumphantly to the leadership of a great nation. Political trickery, or any tampering with the spirit of the conditions under which he had assumed the great charge entrusted to him, was as far removed from his character as the committal of a dishonest action. Of doubtful political expediency there should be none. He would walk straight and upright to the goal, and when the path was blocked with obstacles over which he could not constitutionally pass, he would turn neither to the right nor to the left : would make no attempt to coerce the desires of those who had called him to preside over their destinies. but with honor unscathed abdicate the throne for whose mere lustre he cared so little.

Even those most anxious to bring about the abdication did not withhold their admiration of the disinterestedness of the action, nor deny the loyal and constant observance of a sacred pledge.

CHAPTER VI.

PARLIAMENT opened, as has been said, on April third, in the presence of the King, who on this occasion dispensed with the elaborate ceremonial which had been observed by his predecessors for like functions.

The speech from the Throne was impregnated with a modesty amounting almost to diffidence.

His Majesty assured his hearers of the grateful sentiments, which daily took deeper root in his soul, for the honor conferred upon him, and of his loyal desire to devote himself to the difficult but glorious task which he had voluntarily undertaken; the duties of which he would continue to fulfil, he added, so long

as he possessed the **confidence of** the people
as expressed by **the voice** of their legal representatives. But never, he insisted, would **he**
impose himself on a reluctant majority. **He**
had accepted **the** Crown only after having
been convinced that his action would in no
way affect the peace of Europe. Since his
accession he had received unequivocal tokens
of sympathy from the **various** governments
through their diplomatic representatives **accredited** to his person.

The King expressed his fervent desire **for
the** re-establishment of cordial relations with
the Holy See, for to the Sovereign Pontiff **he,**
as the ruler of an essentially Catholic nation,
must instinctively look **for spiritual** guidance
and comfort.

"When **my** feet touched Spanish **soil,"** exclaimed Amadeus, "I determined to merge my
ideas, my sentiments and **my** interests with
those of the Nation which elected me as its
Head, and whose independent character
would never submit to foreign and illegiti-
mate intrigues."

"Within **the** constitutional limitations I
shall govern with Spain and for Spain, through
the men, **the** ideas and tendencies which are
legally suggested **me** by public opinion as

evinced by Parliamentary majorities—the true
regulators of constitutional monarchies. Convinced of your loyalty, as I am of my own, I
confide to my new country that which I most
love on earth—my family. My sons who,
although they first beheld the light of day on
foreign soil, will have the good fortune to receive their first impressions of life here; their
first language will be Spanish; their education will be in accordance with the customs
of the nation; and from their earliest youth
they will seek inspiration in the examples of
constancy, disinterestedness and patriotism
which are traced in the history of Spain like
luminous stars on the eternal firmament.
Elected by the voice of the country, my
family and I have come to share your joys and
your sorrows alike; to think and feel as you
think and feel; to unite, in short, by imperishable bonds our own fate with the fate
of the people which has confided to me the
direction of its destinies. The task with
which the Nation has associated me is difficult and glorious; perhaps even beyond my
strength, although not without the scope of
my endeavor: but by the help of God, who
is witness to the rectitude of my intentions;
with the concurrence of the Cortes, which

Emmanuel Philibert Present Duke of Aosta

Emmanuel Philibert Present Duke of Aosta

will always be my guide because it expresses
the will of the country ; **and** with the aid of
all honorable men whose co-operation **must**
not be denied me, **I trust** that the united endeavor will obtain as reward the happiness of
the Spanish People."

Although great things could hardly be **expected** from a Parliament in which the government majority did not consist to any great
extent of members of the same party, yet,
nevertheless, **it was** confidently **hoped** that,
yielding **to a** mutual **necessity,** Congress
**would agree on such action as might be
deemed expedient for the** pressing financial
needs, and that pending the **adjustment of
these** party politics **would for the nonce be
left in** abeyance.

The difficulties encountered by the new
régime were complicated **at the outset** by the
knowledge that both in Valencia and **Madrid**
the Carlist and republican factions, without
actually forming a coalition, were, neverthe-
less, in accord ; and by the suspicion, more or
less substantiated by facts, that many officers
in the army had dealings with the Carlists,
which, although of **such** subtle nature as to
defy **detection,** were cunningly calculated to
embarrass the government, and sow the seeds

of discord in the party which had brought the King to power.

In spite of the very moderate expectations founded on the newly elected Cortes, on account of the heterogeneous composition of that body, the friction between its various elements became apparent sooner than was anticipated. Certain celebrations proposed in honor of the pontifical jubilee of Pius IX. gave rise in the Cortes to tumultuous opposition, degenerating into acts of personal violence, and which, spreading to the streets, occasioned serious riots. Angry crowds, incited by agitators of the various political parties who eagerly seized the opportunity of creating disturbances, paraded the streets making hostile demonstrations.

To add to the government's embarrassments Señor Moret finally abandoned his portfolio after repeated attempts to patch up the national finances, which he found in such lamentable confusion that there appeared no remedy less drastic than the suspension of payment of interest on the public debt, and the retention of twenty per cent. on all civil and military salaries.

Señor Sagasta having been prevailed upon, much against his will, to assume, *ad in-*

terim, **the** baneful portfolio **of** finance, **the** Marshal struggled on, vainly trusting to keep his colleagues together by means of temporary expedients. The discord, however, rapidly increased; Martos, Zorrilla and Beranger tendered their resignations, and Marshal Serrano was forced to admit to the Cortes on July 20th that his efforts had failed. It was agreed in the Chamber to suspend the sessions pending the construction of a new ministry, the formation of which was again entrusted by the King **to Serrano.** The Marshal, **in spite of his recent discomfiture,** desired **to renew the attempt of a** ministry of **conciliation,** on **the** condition that Sagasta **should form** part **of it.** Martos and Zorrilla **on the con-** trary would **have nothing** further to **do with** conciliation **as** understood by vague **and** indefinite agreements between men of different parties. They demanded **a** clear and outspoken policy and party **action.** Marshal Serrano having failed **in** his endeavors to bring his late colleagues into accord, the King commissioned Señor Zorrilla to form a government.

A few days later Zorrilla and his cabinet took oath before the King, and, the Cortes having **been** convened, the **new** Premier,

who had retained for himself the direction
of the Ministry of the Interior, made his pro-
fession of faith, in which he declared that he
and his colleagues would adhere to the principles of the old Progressista party, and
that their progamme would be that of the
revolution of September, 1868.

Here at least was a clear and definite declaration of policy. Here also was a government composed of men of the same political
color, and which might reasonably be expected
to promise strength and durability. Yet in
less than two months the vaunted fabric had
crumbled to dust, and Amadeus was again
forced to confront the emergency he was to
become so familiar with during his short
reign. Another Progressista cabinet, with
Zorrilla again at its head, presented itself
before the Cortes; and again the high-sounding assurances of Concord, Liberty and Progress were heard.

A brief respite from the constant worry of
bickering politics was afforded Don Amadeo
in August by a visit from his brother Prince
Humbert. On the arrival of the Italian
Crown Prince the brothers repaired immediately to the Escurial, there to enjoy the quiet
of family life during the few days the visit

was **to last.** On August twenty-seventh the Court returned to Madrid for a **grand** official and diplomatic reception, and review of eighteen thousand troops, **held** in honor of the visiting Prince. On the **30th** Prince Humbert took temporary leave **of the King and** continued his journey to Lisbon, there to **be** the guest **of** his sister, Queen Maria Pia, promising, however, to **join his** brother on his contemplated trip to the provinces.

With the exception of the demands made upon **his time by his** political responsibilities, which **of necessity** were often onerous, **Amadeus remained faithful** in Madrid to the **habits he had contracted in** Italy. He rose at daybreak and went **for** a walk, generally in the Moro gardens, which extend between the palace and the river. This habit of early rising, so contrary to accepted traditions amongst the Spanish aristocracy, occasioned **a** rather ludicrous incident on the morning after the King's arrival in Madrid. At eight o'clock, he having then been up and at work for over two hours, Amadeus called for breakfast. The terrified major-domo, stammering confused excuses, was however forced to admit that nothing had as yet been prepared, as it was not supposed His Majesty would leave

8

his apartments before eleven. Nothing
daunted, Amadeus summoned an aide-de-
camp, and proceeded on foot to a neighboring café where he breakfasted like any other
good citizen.

A favorite morning excursion was to the
museums. On these occasions the King
crossed the city to the Prado on foot, attended by a single aide-de-camp. The servants returning from their early marketing
would relate to their mistresses how they had
met the King, and almost brushed against
him with their baskets full of vegetables and
household provisions.

The democratic simplicity of these excur-
sions gave offence to many, who maintained
that the monarch lowered the majesty of his
office in dispensing with the time-honored
ceremonial of his predecessors. The Carlists
and Alfonsinists sneered at the vagaries of
" King Maccaroni," as they contemptuously
styled him, but all parties united in considering the proceeding hazardous in the extreme.
Nor were they wrong, for in July an unsuccessful attempt was made on his life by an
unknown individual who discharged a pistol
at him as he walked through the streets.
The King was uninjured, and the incident

seemed to make little impression on him; it certainly did not cause him to alter his habits or to mingle less freely with his subjects. But the occurrence justified the anxiety felt by those who were charged with His Majesty's safety.

Amadeus took a boyish delight in shaking off the agents of the secret police who continually dogged his steps under the pretence of affording him protection. On one occasion when leaving the café-concert in the Buen Retiro the King was jostled by some rough-looking characters, and robbed of his watch and purse. Whether this was really the work of criminals, or was perpetrated by the police themselves in order to convince their royal master of the necessity of their precautions, still remains a mystery. At the time, however, the opinion prevailed that the police were not altogether unconnected with the incident, especially as the chiefs had recently rather over-reached themselves in their official zeal by the recovery of a cigarette case supposed to have been lost, but which in reality had never left His Majesty's possession. On this memorable occasion the detectives, desirous of giving evidence of their efficiency but unable to trace the missing property, had quietly duplicated it and triumphantly carried their capture to the palace, there to be met with the disconcerting information that the lost cigarette-case had been found peacefully reposing in the pocket of one of His Majesty's coats which had been thrown aside.

There was much politic talk of confiding the safety of His Majesty's person to the natural courtesy of his subjects, and doubtless his free and unconstrained intercourse with the people did much to disarm insult or possible violence ; nevertheless, in spite of the rather ludicrous incident above related, the really efficient and constant watchfulness of the police was a safeguard which could ill have been dispensed with, distasteful though it was to the Sovereign accustomed to liberty of action and freedom from personal constraint.

On his return to the palace after the morning walk Amadeus received the Captain General and the Governor of Madrid, who, according to ancient custom, must present themselves daily to personally receive the King's orders for the army and police. Then came the ministers. Besides meeting the cabinet once a week at the council for the regular transaction of business, Amadeus received one of its members in turn each day, thus familiarizing himself with the affairs of each separate department. After the minister had retired the audiences began. An hour, more often two, was daily consecrated to this duty. The demands and petitions were innumerable, all tending, however, to the same end : subsidies, pensions, privileges, employment in government service, requests for decorations and the like. To all the King made a practice of listening with marked courtesy although the importunate petitioner must soon have become aware of the annoyance or boredom he was inflicting by the wriggling and shuffling of his victim, one of whose characteristic peculiarities was, when nervous or excited, to stand leaning on a chair through the legs of which he would twist and twine his own long limbs.

The King and Queen generally lunched alone, having at their table a single Lady of Honor and a Chamberlain. After lunch the King smoked one of those long, so-called Virginia cigars, dear to the heart of every Italian officer, and betook himself to his study, there to occupy himself with affairs of state. Nor was the Queen excluded from discussions on matters appertaining to government : especially when dealing with questions of differences of opinion between the ministers, or of reconciliation between party leaders, Amadeus sought her tactful advice and ready intelligence.

The King read many newspapers, irrespective of color or opinion: he himself perused the anonymous epistles condemning him to death, or those offering advice as to how the country should be governed; while his eye also scanned the numerous projects for social renovation submitted by scatter-brained enthusiasts, and the cleverly worded or grossly insulting satirical poetry fresh from the venomous pen of some unknown foe. Political criticism in the press was to be expected, but the personal abuse heaped upon the royal head can only find a parallel in the columns of the opposition papers in the United States at the time of a Presidential election. He might consider himself lucky indeed when it was only his personal appearance which caused dissatisfaction to his subjects; or when fault was found with his gait when walking: or again at his mode of returning a salute. A large portion of the old Spanish nobility practically boycotted the royal couple, and those who dared openly displayed

their aversion by acts of discourtesy in the
public streets and promenades, while in the
salons of the aristocracy the insidious warfare of slander and ridicule was nightly
waged. Outside a narrow circle in which
the brightest stars were the Countess della
Alinma and the Marquis de Ulugares who
had consented to accept positions in the
royal household, and who formed conspicuous
exceptions, those frequenting the Court were
almost entirely officials and politicians. The
Queen felt this isolation most keenly, while it
is reasonable to suppose that the King, although he never for a moment departed from
his habitual reserve, also suffered bitterly
from the scoffing of those whose high social
position should have made them naturally the
staunchest upholders of the royal dignity.

Nearly every afternoon the King was accustomed to ride, followed at a distance of fifty
paces by a single groom in scarlet livery.
The exit of His Majesty from the palace
was heralded by a flourish of trumpets by
the guard as was also his return. Beyond
this simple formality all royal apanage was
dispensed with, and the good people of
Madrid looked in vain for the brilliant cav-
alcade which had clattered after the ex-

Queen Isabella during her progress through the streets of her capital. Alas ! discontent was in the air, and the democratic simplicity of the present order gave as much offence as the extravagant ostentation of the past. In like manner the modest apartment selected by the King and Queen in the huge palace was in marked contrast to the endless suites occupied by the members of the late dynasty. Amadeus reserved three small rooms for his personal use: a study, a bedroom and tiny dressing-room. The bedroom opened on a long corridor which led to the two rooms occupied by the young princes, and to the apartment of the Queen, which in its turn communicated with these. Here the family life of the royal couple was concentrated, the state apartments being used on official occasions only.

Dinner parties were given every Sunday at Court. To these were invited generals, deputies, professors, shining lights from the worlds of Letters, Science and Art, diplomatists, and foreigners of high rank or position. The Queen conversed with all, displaying a knowledge and culture far beyond the limits generally assigned to feminine education, and remarkable both for depth of perception and

accuracy in detail. This was due to the care
of her early training which had been jealously
supervised by her mother, herself a great student and bibliophile. Maria Victoria had read
much and deeply, and had divined life before
knowing it. The young sovereign possessed
the erudition of a German savant: in addition
to **Latin** and Greek she was conversant with
five or six modern languages, and had studied
the higher mathematics even to the extent
of integral and differential calculus. Besides
these **rather** austere accomplishments the
Queen **was an artist and a** musician **of no
mean technical** skill. **Gifted with a rare**
sentiment for criticism, **she** was at once **a**
sympathetic listener and intelligent **performer.**

With these advantages, together with **her**
natural **charm** of face and manner, **it** is little
wonder that the **young sovereign captivated**
those fortunate enough to be received at the
palace. Her Majesty spoke Spanish fluently
and correctly, and took the deepest interest
in the history, literature, art **and** national
customs of her adopted country. It has been
said of her that the only thing needful to make
her a real Spaniard was the desire to remain
in Spain. This desire Maria Victoria never
professed. She had ascended **the** throne

with her husband almost under protest, and
merely because it had been represented to
her that duty lay in that direction.   Writing
to a friend on the eve of her departure for
Spain she says: " We are not going with any
intention of imposing ourselves upon the
country; and the day on which our labors
are proved vain we will return the crown to
those who gave it us."

After the abdication and return to Italy
General Lanza went to Turin to confer with
Amadeus.   On his arrival at the palace at
the hour fixed for the audience the General
was informed that the ex-King had been
unexpectedly obliged to absent himself, but
that Maria Victoria, although indisposed and
confined to her bed, desired to speak with
him, and requested he would go to her.   As
soon as Lanza entered her apartment the
Queen began speaking with great enthusiasm
of the joy she experienced at finding herself
once more in Italy, at rest concerning the
safety of her husband and sons, and after
undergoing such anxiety and terror, to feel
herself surrounded by an atmosphere of peace
and domestic happiness.   Continuing to dwell
on the period spent in Spain she related the
days of her martyrdom with such intensity

of coloring, such variety of **detail** and warmth **of** feeling, that Lanza could only listen in amazement.

In his memoirs, commenting on this conversation the General remarks : " It was **the** Mother and Wife that spoke **in her: the** Queen was **never** manifest, **and her** judgments appeared to me often warped by her personal feelings, and consequently not always just or exact."

Lanza, who held the opinion that Amadeus had too readily yielded **to the** impulse of the moment, or in other words had been **premature** in his abdication, endeavored to **argue this point with the** ex-Queen, **but** failed **to convince her. At last, moved by** admiration **of the** quick intelligence **of his** interlocutor, but yielding to **the** intensity **of his** own **convictions, he** gave utterance **to the** equivocal **remark :** " What **a pity that with so** much intellect there could **not have been** combined **a** little ambition ! **What** an influence such would have exercised **on** the mind **of** the King ! "

But **to** return to Madrid.

The Queen also gave audiences, although **on** account **of** her delicate health **it was not** possible **for her to do so** daily. In the presence of a Chamberlain and Lady of Honor, Her Majesty received all sorts and conditions: from the Court lady in her silks and furs to the factory hand, from the wife of a Minister of State or a deputy in the Cortes, to the loud-voiced woman of the people ; listening to the vapid flattery of the one and to the long tales of misery and pain of the other; offering advice or consolation, or more substantial aid, as required. Besides the hundred thousand francs devoted monthly to charitable purposes, this noble lady gave largely in all directions, and it is estimated that nearly ten millions of her private fortune were thus distributed during the two years of her sojourn in Spain. With the twenty-five thousand francs allowed monthly by the State for the maintenance of the young Prince Emmanuel, Maria Victoria founded a School and Kindergarten for the children of washerwomen who during their working hours were unable to attend to their offspring. This establishment was situated in view of the royal palace. There were to be found recreation grounds, nurseries and a hospital, besides a staff of teachers, nurses and attendants to look after the wants of the little ones. In addition Her Majesty founded an orphan asylum : a refuge

and school for the children of the workers in
the tobacco factory, and a soup kitchen in which
she took a personal and active part, supervising the distribution of soup, meat and bread
to all the poor of the capital who cared to
avail themselves of her bounty. To reach
those unfortunates whose social position, or
pride, forbade their having recourse to such a
public institution, the Queen employed a staff
of sisters of charity who received from her
hands monthly thirty thousand francs.

The organization of these charities is all
the more remarkable when it is remembered
that the royal couple remained in Spain
barely two years.

CHAPTER VII.

ALMOST immediately on the departure of Prince Humbert for Portugal followed that of Amadeus on an official visit to the south-eastern provinces of the Kingdom.

During His Majesty's absence Marshal Serrano was charged with the safety of the young princes and of the Queen, who, owing to slight indisposition, was unable to accompany her husband.

Acting on the advice of his counsellors the King issued a proclamation granting a general amnesty for political offences committed previous to the 31st of July of the preceding year. This sop thrown to the malcontents of all classes would, it was asserted, especially serve to propitiate the Carlists and republicans, many of whom had taken refuge beyond the frontier. In spite of this act of clemency considerable anxiety was felt as to the result of the royal visit to such hot-beds of political intrigue as Valencia and Barcelona, the latter especially noted for its turbulent republican element and insurrectionary tendencies. But the young sovereign was undaunted by the sinister predictions spread abroad, and declared himself determined to appear before his subjects in those commercial centres with the same frank disregard of danger as had been adopted in the capital.

Early on the morning of September second the start was made. The royal train, most luxuriously fitted up for that period, consisted of six carriages communicating one with the other, and including reception saloon, boudoir, bedrooms, dining-saloon, kitchen, and accommodation for the suite. A guard of sixty men picked from the ranks of the Cantabria regiment accompanied His Majesty. Valencia was the first stop of importance, and here the cordiality of the reception offered the Sovereign far surpassed the most sanguine anticipations. It had been an-

nounced that His Majesty would visit the
Cathedral, but on approaching that edifice
the quick eye of Amadeus noticed that it
was intended to slight the dignity of his
office by refraining from the display of ecclesiastical pomp usual on the visit of a monarch.
With ready tact the young ruler caused the
procession to make a detour which brought
him to the door of the sacred shrine of Our
Lady of the Outcasts, most highly venerated
by the inhabitants of Valencia. Making his
way into the church Amadeus knelt unosten-
tatiously amongst the humble worshippers
who thronged the aisle, and on leaving
handed the gold watch he wore to the verger
as an offering to the shrine of the Virgin.

This incident caused a most favorable impression amongst the lower classes of the
population, and when followed up by visits
to the hospitals and various municipal charitable institutions, completely turned the tide
of popular sentiment.

It was, however, at the bull-ring, whither
Amadeus now repaired to witness the skill
of Bocanegra and the famous Lagartijo, that
popular enthusiasm reached a climax. It so
happened that El Tato, a torero of great
popularity whose daring in the ring had re-

cently cost him a leg, was seated in the audience sadly contemplating the feats of his former rivals. Amadeus, hearing of his presence, immediately sent for the disabled torero, and, in full view of the seventeen thousand spectators, warmly grasped his hand and presented him with his cigar-case. No action could have gone more directly to a Spaniard's heart. The success of the visit to Valencia was assured.

The royal entry into Barcelona was witnessed by crowds which saluted the King respectfully if not enthusiastically; while the official festivities were on a scale worthy of the importance of the great industrial interests represented. A drenching rain greeted the visitors on their arrival, without, however, in any way interfering with the programme. After a stay of a few days fully occupied with the usual inspection of hospitals, charitable institutions, factories and expositions, the King started on a short visit to Gerona and other places of minor importance.

In spite of the beneficial effects anticipated by the royal clemency the most stringent precautionary measures for the safety of the Sovereign had everywhere been enforced. In towns where the loyalty of the inhabitants was doubtful the garrisons were doubled and trebled; care being taken that only trusted troops, commanded by officers whose attachment to the monarchy was above suspicion, should be employed. Thus the journey, if not a continual ovation, at least passed off without unpleasant incident, with the exception of Saragossa, where an officious Mayor received His Majesty with a speech the transparent impertinence of which Don Amadeus averted by a quick and tactful answer which turned the tables on the over-confident official, who meekly followed in the wake of the triumphal entry he had warned the Sovereign not to expect.

On September twentieth Amadeus returned to Barcelona to meet his brother Humbert, who, after leaving Portugal, had visited Seville and Granada, and was now on his way back to Italy. Together the brothers, on foot and unattended, explored the town, entering the cafés like private citizens, and mingling freely with the populace. An expedition was also made to the famous monastery of Monserrat, where a magnificent Te Deum was executed in their honor, and where the reception was one of marked sympathy and cordiality.

On the departure of the Italian Prince the return journey to Madrid was begun. Lerida and Saragossa were successively visited, and pains taken to arrange a personal interview at Logroño with the aged Espartero.

Particular importance was attached to the meeting between the young Sovereign and this revered hero and popular idol, who had, on more than one occasion, held the destinies of the nation in his hand, and whose influence and prestige were still immense. As the royal train steamed into the gaily decorated station of Logroño the excitement was intense, while every eye was strained to catch a glimpse of the meeting between the glorious veteran and his youthful Sovereign.

Espartero greeted the King with dignified affection, uttering the following words of welcome :

" Sire : Everywhere the people greet Your Majesty with patriotic enthusiasm because they recognize in the young monarch the most staunch upholder of the liberty and independence of their country, and are convinced that if their enemies try to destroy them, Your Majesty, at the head of the army, and the metropolitan militia, will confound and scatter them, guiding us always in the path of honor and glory. Sire : My failing health did not permit me to have the honor of personally congratulating Your Majesty and your August Consort in Madrid on your accession to the throne of Saint Ferdinand. To-day I reiterate that I loyally welcome Your Majesty as King of Spain, on whom this supreme dignity has been conferred by the national will. Sire : In this town I own a modest dwelling which I now offer to Your Majesty, begging you to honor it with your presence. My wife makes Your Majesty the same offer, and begs me to respectfully salute you."

The royal visit was attended with unqualified popular enthusiasm from start to finish. Crowds arrived from neighboring towns and villages, drawn to Logroño as much by curiosity to see the popular hero as to welcome the new King, but according to both unstinted applause and affectionate consideration.

A few months later in commemoration of the first anniversary of his accession Amadeus added to the dignities bestowed upon Espartero, the title of Prince of Vergara, in memory of the peace concluded between the liberals and Carlists.

On October first, Amadeus again entered

his capital, **just in time** to **assist at** the ministerial **crisis brought** about by the discussion concerning **the election of the** President of the Chamber of Deputies.

Although Zorrilla and Sagasta had been close political friends, the latter **soon** broke away from the partisans **of** his former ally, who were too inclined to radicalism to **coincide** with the views he then held. Señor Zorrilla, who owed his power to **the aid of** the radicals, and was especially **under obligations** to Señor Rivero, would **gladly** have seen **the** latter in the President's **chair. His adversaries, however,** wished **the place for Sagasta and** were prepared to fight **for their opinions.** The movement had already assumed such importance that **it was felt that** should Sagasta be elected it **would be** tantamount to a ministerial defeat. Espartero was called upon **to** attempt to patch up the differences existing between the leaders, but refused to mix himself up in the affair. As had been anticipated the government candidate **was** defeated in the session of October third by a vote of **113 to 123,** and Sagasta was duly proclaimed President of the Chamber. Zorrilla then and there declared **his** inability to carry on the government, and he and his colleagues presented their resignations to the King. Although the resignations were accepted by Amadeus, many of Señor Zorrilla's most fervent partisans were not willing to acknowledge themselves beaten, and attempted to foment a public demonstration which was to manifest the unshaken popular faith in Zorrilla, and the desire to have him and his colleagues continue in office. About a thousand adherents were enlisted for this purpose, who paraded the streets making special disturbance beneath the palace windows, loudly calling on the King to show himself. Amadeus wisely refrained from lending himself to any popular manifestation, although he strenuously endeavored to enable the conflicting parties to arrive at some understanding. Appeal was again made to Espartero to use his very considerable influence, but the old statesman piteously begged to be left in peace.

Meanwhile a tumultuous rabble surrounded the Queen's carriage as she was returning from a drive, and loudly bawled: "Death to Sagasta! Long live the radical ministry! Zorrilla or a radical republic!"

Her Majesty, greatly alarmed, was forced to make some reply, which she did with quiet dignity : **but the emotion** and nervous strain **were such that** she fainted on entering the **palace.**

Finally Admiral Malcampo, **one of Prim's** old lieutenants, was prevailed upon **to attempt** the formation of a cabinet, and actually succeeded, with the exercise **of** great prudence and tact, in gathering around him colleagues who were acceptable to the Zorrillam and **capable of** working with both parties. The new ministry took oath before the King on October sixth.

The closing months of this first year of the reign of Amadeus **were fraught with many dangers and trials, not the least of which was** the impetus given **by the Zorrilla-Sagasta** controversy **to the Carlist insurrection. In vain** were members **of this party imprisoned,** and **the** death **penalty** threatened against **those** caught in arms. **A threat** rarely carried out, as reprisals were feared on the many military prisoners in the hands of the rebels, and it being moreover the policy of the government to show clemency **whenever** practicable. A state of **siege** was proclaimed **in** all the provinces most contaminated, and **military** operations strenuously pursued. **Don** Carlos himself **rarely** appeared in **the field,**

preferring the prudent security of the French frontier. Battles there were none: the tactics of the Carlists being those of guerilla warfare. In vain did the government troops endeaver to engage the enemy: the bands melted away on the approach of the regulars, only to reform after rapid forced marches, and harass their flank, or cleverly lead their detachments into ambush. In some instances the promise of free pardon led rebel chiefs to lay down their arms and disband their men, but the vengeance wreaked upon such by late comrades was so terrible that few dared avail themselves of the terms offered.

Meanwhile the financial situation grew daily more complicated, while the jealousies and friction in the Cortes made any radical or permanent amelioration impossible.

Under these conditions, although the word failure was not yet uttered aloud, the first year of the reign closed with a very general feeling of uneasiness, intensified in Court circles by a presentiment of greater evils to come.

CHAPTER VIII.

THE year 1872, which was to prove so eventful, opened quietly enough.

On January first, the King listened to the optimistic assurances of his ministers, and responded to the congratulatory addresses of deputations from both Houses of Parliament. Neverthless there seemed little enough subject for congratulation by those who reviewed the political situation dispassionately and with understanding. The country was on the brink of bankruptcy: the hold of the government over the Cortes was gradually slipping away; while the Carlist insurrection, far from being quelled, was fiercer and bolder than ever.

In April His Majesty nominated Marshal
Serrano Commander in Chief of the troops
charged with the duty of repressing the
growing insurrection : an appointment which
resulted in the much-commented convention of Amorevieta. According to the stip-
ulations of this extraordinary document not
only was a general amnesty proclaimed
for those insurgents who should lay down
their arms, but the officers of the regular
army who had deserted their colors and
passed over to the enemy were to be reinstated
in the rank they had previously held. A vote
of censure in the Cortes caused the fall of
the Sagasta ministry on May 27, and Marshal
Serrano, in view of the dissatisfaction his
measure produced, was constrained to resign,
not only his military command, but also the
presidency of the council of ministers, both
of which charges he however speedily resumed, yielding, we are told, to the pressure
brought to bear on him by the King and his
former colleagues.

With singularly accurate prognostication
General Sickles, then American Minister to
Spain, observes in his despatch to his government, dated Madrid, June 8, 1872: " The
new cabinet takes office in the presence of the

most **critical** situation yet confronted by **the
present** dynasty. The King has unfortu-
nately **alienated** the friendship of the party
that placed him on the throne. The various
elements of the opposition, re-enforced by this
defection **of the** radicals under Zorrilla, become bolder in their demands every day. The
Carlists are still in the field in great numbers.
It is true that several bands availed them-
selves of the generous terms **of** surrender
granted by Marshal Serrano at Amorevieta,
but the rising is by no means pacificated even
in the Pyrenees, and it is said to be taking
serious proportions in Catalonia. The republicans are kept tranquil **by the** firm attitude
of their leaders, who are understood, however,
only to await a **more favorable** moment **for a**
hostile demonstration. The **radical chief,**
Mr. Zorrilla, has retired from the Chamber **of**
Deputies, and renounced the parliamentary
leadership **of** the progressista democrats, to
which he succeeded on the death of General
Prim. . . . The indications at this moment
incline me to the opinion that the present dynasty has seen its best days. It will be probably succeeded before long by **a** provisional
government, in which the republicans, largely
re-enforced from the ranks of the radicals, will

contend with the partisans of the young Prince Alfonso for supremacy. If Marshal Serrano should be reconciled to the old dynasty by the offer of the regency during the minority of Alfonso, or if he were satisfied with the concession of the regency to his friend the Duke of Montpensier, the uncle of the Prince, such an arrangement might hold out a fair promise of success; nevertheless it cannot be doubted that the republicans have much to justify their anticipated triumph. The failure of the monarchical parties to satisfy the exigencies of the country, or even the requirements of a successful party organization; the prevailing belief in the necessity of reforms which can only be effected by a revolution more thorough than that of 1868; the apparent incompatability between the democratic constitution adopted in 1869, representing the advanced ideas of this epoch, and the monarchy ingrafted on it as a concession to Spanish traditions; the profound disappointment of the liberal party in the results of their effort to reconcile the throne with a government essentially popular and free outside of the executive department; the inability of the country to maintain the enormous expenditure entailed upon it by the monarchical establishment, and its accessories in the Army, Church, and **Civil list; and** last, **not** least, the stability **of the** popular situation represented in France by Monsieur Thiers— these, and other considerations **I** need not mention, support the views of those who predict that the successor of Amadeus may be **a** President chosen by the Spanish People."

" The suffrages of the people of this country **are** divided mainly between the Carlists, the radicals, and the republicans. The first is **the** party of tradition and **reaction.** In the rural portions **of Spain it is especially strong, and it counts on the support** of the larger **part of the** clergy. **The towns are** nearly all **radical or** republican. **Outside of the army** and navy, **and a circle of clever** politicians supported by **a** goodly **number** of persons in office or on the pension **list, there is no** considerable popular strength belonging **to** the conservative party led by Marshal Serrano, The late dynasty has few advocates outside of a fraction of the aristocracy which has little influence in Spanish politics. **It** is said, however, that several battalions of the army have been gained over to the cause of the Prince Alfonso **by** means often found effectual in the Spanish military service.

"If we pass beyond the frontier, it is easy to see that France takes little pains to conceal the indifference with which she regards the fortunes of the present dynasty. The alliance understood to exist between the King of Italy and the German Emperor is a sufficient explanation of this coolness, without assuming that France desires a republican neighbor. Apart from the German sympathies of the reigning house, it is perhaps more in accord with England than any of the other Powers, as you must have observed from the hesitation of the British cabinet to second our earnest appeals to Spain for the abolition of slavery and for a more humane colonial policy."

Although General Sickles, with a clear political insight rare even in a trained diplomacy, proved himself in several instances a reliable prophet, exception must be taken to the statement concerning " the inability of the country to maintain the enormous expenditure entailed upon it by the monarchical establishment, and its accessories in the army, church and civil list." The expenditure for the army must have continued no matter under what form of government; Amadeus could certainly not be held accountable for the expenses entailed by a Church established centuries before **his** advent; the amount fixed for the civil **list** by the Delegation which offered the crown **to** the Prince at Florence was six million pesetas (a little over a million of dollars). When the first instalment of the civil list came due, on the arrival of Amadeus in Spain, the King exclaimed: " Give it to **the** school-masters whose salaries have **not** been paid for fifteen months ! "

We have seen **the extreme** simplicity **of** the Court life ; no president could have **ab**stained more completely from ostentation **or** display. On the advent **of** the Italian couple **the national finances were in a lamentable** condition, and **if circumstances over** which **he** could have **no possible control** obliged the **King to leave** them in **the same** deplorable state, it was certainly not his personal expenditure, or the cost of **the** maintenance of the Court, which was to blame. Spain had been for two years before the Prince's election **to** the Throne passing through a revolution—alway an expensive luxury, in many cases **a** ruinous one—while for the two years he remained at the head **of** the government revolution continued to drain the Treasury. **It** may be contended that it was the presence of

a foreigner on the throne which caused the
continuance of the revolution. But suppos-
ing a republic to have been established in
1870, or a regency proclaimed until such time
as Alfonso should be of age to rule, is it likely
that the Carlist insurrection would not have
taken place merely because the government
went under a different name? Hardly. It
is easy enough for those reviewing the political situation of 1870 to 1873 in the light of
events which have transpired in the last
twenty years, to moralize as to what might
have been. But we most not overlook the
fact that at the time of the accession of Amadeus popular sentiment, as expressed in the
Constituent Cortes, was dead against the
return of the Spanish Bourbons. The events
of 1868 were too recent, and political passions
ran too high, to attach more than a sentimental value to the prophecy which placed
a descendant of Isabella on the Throne.
Although then as now the advocates for the
republic raved and stormed, time has proved
that Spain could give no guarantee of stability for that form of government, probably
the most intricate, certainly the most beset
with peril to an emotional race whose
susceptible hereditary pride forms the

very keynote of their national characteristics.

Far from benefiting in a pecuniary sense from their exalted station, the representatives of the House of Savoy left millions of their private fortune in Spain. If the honor conferred upon Amadeus and his Consort was great, so was the expense attendant thereon.

Writing a few days later, the American diplomatist informs his government that:

" The cabinet of Marshal Serrano left office after the very brief tenure, even in Spain, of seven days. It appears that, in view of the extremely critical state of affairs reported in my No. 388, the President of the Council of Ministers advised the King that it was necessary to suspend those articles of the constitution guaranteeing personal rights. His majesty declined to sanction this measure, and declared that when he found he could no longer rule in accordance with the constitution he had sworn to maintain, he would resign his office. The announcement of this decision to the Council of Ministers over which His Majesty presided was followed by their resignation on the spot. The King did not hesitate a moment in accepting the

10

situation thus suddenly presented, and, until an hour afterward, when Admiral Topete, the minister of marine, surprised the Chamber of Deputies with a brief statement of what had occurred, no intimation of a cabinet crisis had transpired."

" Remarkable as Spain is for political changes, nobody was prepared for the transformation that followed. The King went through the customary form of consulting the presiding officers of the two Houses of Congress, both of whom belong to the conservative party, and, putting aside their advice, immediately sent for Lieutenant-General Fernandez de Cordova, the leader of the radicals since the recent withdrawal of Mr. Ruiz-Zorrilla from politics, who was asked to form a cabinet."

After consulting with the leaders of the radical party General de Cordova agreed to attempt to carry on the government provided Señor Zorrilla be named President of the Council, and that the existing Cortes, chosen under the auspices of Señor Sagasta, should be dissolved and new elections ordered. These arrangements having been accepted by the Crown, the ministry was definitely constituted.

"It must be admitted, states General Sickles, in the same despatch from which the above has been quoted, that this ministry takes office in the presence of the gravest difficulties. On the first of next month the half-yearly interest on the public debt, amounting in round numbers to twenty-five millions of dollars, becomes due, and there is not a dollar in the treasury to pay it. The financial situation in Cuba is so critical that it causes even more disquietude than the insurrection, which remains defiant at the close of the fourth campaign. The Carlists' revolt holds out in the north against an army of twenty-two thousand regular troops. General Morion, lately assigned to the command of these forces, is the third officer who has filled that post within three months. In Catalonia, called the New England of Spain, for the thrift, industry and independence of its inhabitants, the Carlists' movement is combining so rapidly that General Baldrich, lately appointed to the command of the forces operating in that principality, demands a re-enforcement of no less than ten thousand men. The Duke of Montpensier announces to-day his reconciliation with the Spanish Bourbons, represented by his nephew the young Prince

Alfonso, and this publication is accompanied by a manifesto signed by two hundred and thirty generals, deputies, senators and grandees of Spain, in favor of the Prince, with Montpensier as regent. And although the republican leaders still restrain the impatience of the great body of that party, professing a purpose to pause awhile longer, at least until the struggle between the several monarchical elements becomes yet more pronounced, there is, nevertheless, a numerous body of republicans following the counsels of the 'Igualdad' and the 'Combate,' two of the most popular journals of that party, who insist on taking arms and trying their fortunes in the civil war that seems unhappily to be inaugurated." . . . " It remains to be seen whether the radical ministry, summoned at the eleventh hour to the councils of the King, can deal with a situation so grave, and for which they need not only statesmen, but military talent of no common order. The main current of public opinion runs in their favor. The prestige of the Crown is once more on their side. They lose no time in taking advantage of an opportunity afforded by the resignation of nearly all the incumbents of the principal offices to fill the vacant places with their partisans, thus securing the large and profitable patronage of the Spanish Government. They promise, through their newspaper organs, to put in operation at once a series of reforms, embracing a large reduction of expenditures, the suppression of useless offices, the separation of Church and State, the abolition of conscription for the regular army, trial by jury, the emancipation of slavery, and the extension of the Spanish constitution to the colonies. Whether these promises will be kept, whether, if fulfilled, the resistance such a development of the programme of the revolution of 1868 must encounter will be overcome by the support it should bring to the party that has the courage and the constancy to undertake it in earnest, I shall not venture to predict."

CHAPTER IX.

FOR some time past Amadeus had received
warning that a plot was rife for a fresh attempt upon his life, and it was rumored
that the night of July eighteenth had been
selected for the perpetration of some outrage.
Nevertheless the King refused to alter in any
degree his usual habits, and resolved to spend
that evening in the society of his subjects.
Whether the decision was born of his inherent
contempt of danger, or from the conviction
that it especially behoved him to show himself to his people at a time when such rumors were in circulation, who shall say! It
would appear, however, that on this occasion
Amadeus did not place much faith in the
warnings of a police he had ample reason to

believe officious, or give credence to the existence of any serious danger, since he allowed the Queen to accompany him.

Their Majesties spent the hot, close, evening listening to the concert in the public gardens of the Buen Ritiro, one of Madrid's most famous pleasure-grounds. At midnight, on the close of the concert, the homeward drive was begun along the route where, on account of the evil reports abroad, constables had been stationed at intervals sufficiently apart to avoid the suggestion that special precautions had been deemed necessary.

As the royal carriage proceeded at a rapid pace up the via del Arenal, a broad, modern thoroughfare, a public vehicle, adopting the same tactics as those which had been employed in the assassination of General Prim, attempted to impede its progress by driving at right angles across the street, and fouling the Court equipage. Fortunately, however, the King's coachman was able to knock the cab-driver from his box before the wheels of the two vehicles became locked. At the same moment six or seven shots were fired from the midst of a group of idlers standing on the corner. The King sprang to his feet at the first detonation, shouting :

"Here is the King. Fire at him, not at the others!"

The aide-de-camp, seated in front of Their Majesties, courageously threw himself before the Queen, interposing his body between Her Majesty and the direction from whence the shots were fired.

By a miracle none of the occupants of the carriage were touched, although one of the horses was wounded and the carriage itself riddled with bullets. The postilion immediately whipped up his maddened beasts to full gallop, guiding them in the direction of the palace.

Meanwhile the police closed in on the band of would-be assassins who defended themselves with revolvers. Crowds rapidly assembled and, while impeding the operations of the police, facilitated the escape of many of those implicated in the plot. Two were arrested on the spot; a third killed while desperately attempting to cut his way through. During the night some twenty arrests were made, amongst the most notable of which was that of a certain Dudascal, the ex-chief of an unsavory political association.

The indignation of the populace at the

dastardly attempt was general and widespread. Angry crowds demanded that the prisoners be given into their hands in order that summary justice might be meted out to them. Frightened and excited officials flocked to the palace where they huddled together in the antechambers exchanging vivid and grossly exaggerated accounts of the occurrence. Señor Zorilla was amongst the first to arrive, and was at once ushered into the presence of the King. In spite of the trying ordeal just passed through, Amadeus appeared perfectly calm and collected as he quietly related the circumstances of the attack, and gave orders concerning the measures he desired carried out. His first thought was for his father, and the desire to spare him unnecessary anxiety should exaggerated accounts of the attempted assassination first reach him. Accordingly the following somewhat laconic telegram was immediately despatched to the Italian Court:

"I inform Your Majesty that this evening we were objects of an outrage. Thanks to God are absolutely unhurt. AMADEUS.
"MADRID, July 18,
"1 : 24 A. M."

This message reached Victor Emmanuel while on one of his favorite hunting expeditions in the mountains above Valsavaranche, near Aosta. Rapidly descending to the nearest encampment to which the telegraph wires had been carried for his convenience, the King, in spite of his terrible anxiety, forwarded congratulations and words of encouragement to his son; at the same time urging him to loyally persevere in the task he had undertaken, and to show to the world that a prince of the House of Savoy, at any cost, and regardless of personal peril, would pursue the aim in view without swerving a hair's breadth from his constitutional obligations.

The following morning Amadeus might have been seen walking without escort through the Madrid streets as if he were as free from worry or danger as the meanest of his subjects.

The Queen, however, did not so readily recover from the recent shock, or close her eyes to the peril of their position. Her Majesty's life was one of continual dread for the safety of her husband and those most dear to her. Each time Amadeus left the palace she suffered torments of apprehension lest he should not enter it again alive.

" Alas ! " the poor lady exclaimed to one
of her intimate friends shortly after the July
outrage, "all here have the right to complain except ourselves. We must bear all in
silence." Her discouragement and mental
anxiety added in no small degree to her consort's distaste for a task, the ultimate accomplishment of which became daily more doubtful.

Amadeus was not the man to allow
questions of personal safety to distract his
mind from public affairs. Amongst the questions to which he had given especial attention,
and the one which most intensely interested
him, was the emancipation of slavery in the
islands of Cuba and Porto Rico. For many
months this problem, bristling with the conflicting elements of vested interest, deep-
rooted custom, humanity and political intrigue, had been occupying the sessions of
the Cortes. The Government was pledged
to reforms colonial and domestic ; but the
difficulty lay in the mode and period of their
accomplishment.

In the autumn of 1872 the question had
reached an acute stage demanding prompt
solution. The members of the cabinet were
agreed in principle but divided in form—three

being for gradual and five for the immediate
abolishment of slavery. It was desired to
immediately introduce in Porto Rico the abolition of slavery as well as certain civil and
municipal reforms, the result of engagements
contracted by the radical party with the
public opinion of Spain, the peaceful condition of the island rendering it feasible;
and it was moreover deemed that this action
would demonstrate the future policy of the
radical party in Cuba as soon as the pacification of the latter—then in the midst of insurrection—should have been accomplished.
On August 5 Amadeus had signed at San
Sebastian regulations dealing with the
emancipation law in both islands, but the
political situation made it inexpedient to then
press the matter before the Cortes. The act
calling out forty thousand men for military
service by conscription was causing considerable discontent. Although the army and
navy had heretofore been supplied in this way,
the measure now provoked unusual opposition, and aroused some of the malcontents in
Andalusia to acts of open hostility. Taken
in conjunction with the firm stand made by
the Carlists and the inability of the government troops to do more than hold the forces

of the Pretender in check, as well as with the insurrection in Cuba which demanded continual reinforcements from the mother country for its suppression, the new movement might well create serious embarrassment to the Crown.

On November 30 a ministerial crisis was narrowly averted. A majority of the ministers had voted for immediate abolition of slavery in Porto Rico, a resolution the minority could not accept. In view of the existing military and political situation, and the necessity of completing the pending conscription, it was decided that the resignation of the Minister of War could not then be accepted, while for reasons of equal gravity it was desirable that the Minister of Finance should await final action on his budget. Under these circumstances it seemed expedient to delay the presentation to the Cortes of the project of the law for immediate emancipation. On the other hand, delay might mean defeat. Irreconcilable differences between Señor Zorrilla and his supporters in Congress were imminent, these alienations were said to be the result of the excessive deference shown by the President of the Council to palace influences. The President of the Cortes him-

self only gave reluctant and half-hearted
support to the Premier, and that only from
a sense of personal obligation, he having been
largely instrumental in persuading Señor
Zorrilla, in the previous June, to renounce
his intention of abandoning political life, and
deciding him to accept the King's invitation
to form a radical ministry.

Yet, in spite of the growing conviction that
neither the ministry, or even the throne, could
long resist the current setting against both,
the issue had to be squarely faced, and those
in sympathy with the Government prepared
for war to the knife.

The crisis was precipitated by Señor Cisa,
a member of the Chamber of Deputies, who
rose in his seat on December ninth to ask for
information concerning the report that the
Government had authorized the sale of slaves
taken from the Cuban insurgents, and of
such as were not indispensable for the maintenance of embargoed estates. Although the
Colonial minister denied the truth of the
assertion, and gave satisfactory evidence as
to the true nature of the transaction which had
given rise to the rumor, the ball once set
rolling, the enemies of the Government's policy were not slow to take advantage of the

opportunity offered. A league was formed to defeat what was described as the terrible dangers which threatened the national integrity in the colonies, through the reckless projects of reform the Government had instituted. Such men as the Duke de la Torre, Admiral Topete, Señor Sagasta, Romero Robledo, Ayala, Balagver and others who, as members of previous cabinets, had declared themselves in favor of the very measures of colonial reform now announced by Señor Zorrilla's administration, gave proof of the most unqualified inconsistency by now joining the league formed for their defeat.

The "Imparcial" of December 16, 1872, reproducing extracts from the reply to the speech from the Throne, read in the Chamber on May 24, 1871, and signed by all the names above quoted, soundly rates the owners thereof.

The passage referred to reads as follows:

"The civil war that to-day rages in Cuba is a fatal legacy of the old régime, under which rancorous passions fermented and prepared the way for an outburst; but the Congress of Deputies shares with Your Majesty the hope that it may be speedily terminated. The firmness of the Government, the patriotism, valor, and endurance of the navy, the army, and the volunteers, the skill of their chiefs, and the continued earnestness of the whole nation, will all contribute to this end, when joined to the conviction that must at last reach the minds of the rebels that by their submission they will attain liberties they seek in vain to win by force. The resort to this only hinders the fulfilment of the promises of the revolution, the *complete realization* of which will doubtless not be much longer deferred by Congress *in the other great Spanish Antilla*, where peace has not been disturbed, and where the *full enjoyment* of political rights and the abolition of Slavery cannot exert a disturbing influence."

As far as the reported address is concerned, it should be remembered that during the whole course of the debate thereon, the proposition of the committee with respect to colonial reforms was in no manner whatever impugned by the conservatives. The Carlists and Moderados alone denied that the Cuban war was " a fatal legacy of the old régime." One hundred and sixty-four deputies signed the address : eighty-five conservatives who now defended the opposite of what they voted for, and seventy-nine radicals who now were simply fulfilling what they then offered to do. "It is therefore demonstrated," continues the "Imparcial," "and demonstrated to conviction, by a simple reading of the foregoing extracts, that the conservatives of to-day do not follow the same conduct or defend the same principles touching the concrete question of the colonies, as they followed and defended in the months of May and June, 1871. . . . Either one of two things. Either the conservatives drafted, voted, and supported the paragraph from the address which we have quoted because they thought it laid down the most patriotic course in the colonies, or they prepared it, voted for it, and defended it, believing the contrary, and secretly resolving not to put it in practice."

The American Minister, reporting these events to his government, writes: ". . . It has seldom happened in the history of Spanish colonial administration that a cabinet has so boldly confronted an organized and powerful resistance to colonial reform. It is not too much to say that during the past three weeks all Spain has been moved by the agitation got up by the partisans of the old colonial régime. The opposition has employed every resource and tried all means to baffle and

11

intimidate the government. All the reactionary parties have rivalled each other in crying 'Danger to Spanish unity!' " Our colonies are lost!' 'Treason in the palace!' Meetings have been held in all the principal towns, under the auspices of societies interested in the trade with the colonies. Agents of the slaveholders in Cuba and Porto Rico have been busy in all kinds of appliances intended to gain over or silence the friends of emancipation. A formidable combination of newspapers, comprising five-sixths of the journals in the capital, and many in the provinces, have become the clamorous organs of the slaveholders. A shower of petitions, letters and telegrams from all parts of the country is represented as an outburst of popular feeling against reform. From Cuba comes the announcement, by cable, that seventy thousand volunteers unite in the demand that no reforms be granted to Porto Rico while an insurgent survives in Cuba. The leaders of all the opposition parties, except the republicans, have met and formed a 'league' to defend the national domain. And finally, on Wednesday night last, the 11th instant, the capital was made the scene of an armed demonstration in the streets, the insurgents crying, ' Down with the filibusterers!' and firing on the police and the troops, several of whom were killed. One of the bands attacked the carriage of the Prime Minister, in which he was supposed to be driving, and mortally wounded a lackey alongside of the coachman, the occupant of the coach, a deputy, narrowly escaping. This outbreak lasted several hours, and was not quelled until a good many of the rioters were shot or bayoneted. An attempt was made to give this seditious movement the appearance of 'a republican rising;' but the instantaneous and indignant denunciation of the act by all the republican chiefs, and the circumstances that the prisoners taken and those who fell in the struggle with the police and the troops were clothed in rags and yet had their pockets well filled with money, the obvious price of their service, quickly betrayed the real origin of the outrage. The appearance of the first of the series of the promised reforms in the face of so much opposition and in defiance of threats and force, has exasperated while it has disappointed the 'league.' Agitation is renewed with unshaken determination and zeal. The next demonstration is to be made in the

Cortes, and another at the palace is to follow. . . . Under all these circumstances, in presence of a resistance not unlike that encountered by Charles the Fifth when he undertook to restrain the usurpations and greed of his viceroys in America. I cannot but applaud the firmness and dignity so far shown by His Majesty's Government in dealing with the difficult questions of colonial reform on a basis consistent with justice and the provisions of the Spanish constitution."

In spite of the tremendous opposition and pressure exercised by the "league" Amadeus was firm in his resolve to support his ministers to the utmost limit of his constitutional powers, and in this again disappointed the members of the opposition, who confidently believed the King would yield when the magnitude of the movement became apparent.

A new force, however, coming from an unexpected quarter, now appeared in the ranks of the abolitionists. Emilio Castelar assumed on this occasion the attitude of an ally of the Government, and threw the weight of his magnificent eloquence in the scale.

General Sickles reports that many ministerial adherents hesitated to follow the Government in their radical colonial policy, and that the slavery party boasted that as many as ninety ministerialists would either dodge the vote or side with the opposition when the appeal to the Chambers was made. Castelar, therefore, while satisfying the exigencies of the republican leadership, must take ground on which he could rally all the liberals of the Chamber—monarchists and republicans. This he did in a masterly manner, scoring an immense parliamentary triumph. "The orator carried the whole house with him," writes General Sickles. "If here and there a few yet lingered in doubt, the enthusiasm of the tribunes and the applause of the Chamber swept them along with the torrent of feeling set in motion by this incomparable speaker."

The result was gall and wormwood to the "league."

In deference to the usual form of procedure the Minister of State was the last to speak, and when he rose it was merely to give utterance to the following graceful tribute: "The debate is closed. Señor Castelar has spoken the last word—the slaves in Porto Rico are already free. The bill the Government will bring in can only give legal sanction and form to the inspired utterance of the world's greatest orator."

CHAPTER X.

As had been anticipated the debate cost the Government the resignations of the Ministers of the Colonies and of Finance, who were not prepared to follow their colleagues on ground of so treacherous a nature. The Minister of War, however, although not fully in accord with his colleagues, agreed to retain his portfolio temporarily pending the accomplishment of certain military reforms.

In announcing these resignations to the Senate Señor Zorrilla stated: "I could do nothing else than go to His Majesty the King and explain the situation of the cabinet to him, and it was equally my duty, although His Majesty was cognizant of the question

from the first, to set before him the full
gravity of the issue and the responsibility
that would rest on any government that
might decide it. I went to confer with His
Majesty at noon yesterday, and told him that
a cabinet council was convened for nine
o'clock that night, and that if, at that hour,
I had no commands from him in a contrary
sense to that in which I thought the crisis
should be settled, I would, on the following
day, lay before him the resignations of those
ministers who were not in accord with the majority of the cabinet, replacing them with
proper substitutes. I had the honor and the
satisfaction to hear from His Majesty's lips
how great was his regret that a new crisis had
arisen; but, at the same time, I had the pleasure to hear that in the divergence of views
common to all parties, while esteeming all opinions as sincere, he chose the most liberal and
the most humane; and His Majesty charged
me that whatever reforms should be attempted
should be the work of the Parliament; that
the glory of the reforms should belong to
Parliament, while the Government should
bear whatever responsibility might result.

Señor Zorrilla then proceeded to give em-
phatic denial to the accusations brought

against the Government that the cabinets of
Rome, Berlin and England used their influence against the legitimate interests of Spain.
The day was past, the Minister urged, when
foreign powers could say to Spanish Ambassadors that they merely represented the
Queen's personal wishes. He acknowledged
the reforms were approved in certain high
quarters, and undoubtedly the English, Italian, and other governments were interested in wiping out the stain of slavery; but
it was preposterous to allege that any foreign government had attempted to exercise
pressure or influence on the " indomitable
Spanish nation." It must be recollected that
the Government at present merely proposed
the abolition of slavery in Porto Rico: in
Cuba nothing could be done except answer
the voice of the muskets by the roar of cannon. The Government's colonial policy was
based on this distinction; for Cuba, where
there was war, soldiers and money; for Porto
Rico, where there was peace, laws and reforms.
The reforms granted to Porto Rico would undoubtedly influence the situation in Cuba to
the advantage of the Government, and tend
to end the war.

It was well known in political circles that

the United States Government lost no opportunity of advancing the cause of emancipation in the West Indies, while it was, moreover, freely asserted that the United States Minister at Madrid held pledges from the Zorrilla cabinet that reforms, at least as far as Porto Rico was concerned, should be speedily undertaken. The President of the Cortes himself was aware of the pressure brought to bear by the American representative, and what is more approved of it. Señor Rivero considered the radical ministry pledged to proceed with the reforms in Porto Rico, not only in the eyes of their country, but in those of the civilized world.

In his speech on the same subject on March 21, 1873, Señor Castelar admitted that the slavery question was, in reality, an international question. "But," he continued, "notwithstanding that it is an international question, at the time it was brought up by the Zorrilla cabinet it was not, and had not been, the ground of any foreign representations whatever. Its presentation by that cabinet was a free and spontaneous act, requested or demanded by no outside Power. "Yet, the orator proceeds to state in the same speech, "frankness, which in such matters is the best policy, leads me to say that all, absolutely all, the cabinets of Spain have been approached by England. There has not been a single session of the English Parliament that has not found fault with our administration in Cuba, nor a single English minister who has not preferred some claim against us."

It is inconceivable that Señor Castelar should at that time have been ignorant of the nature of the confidences exchanged between Señor Zorrilla and the United States Minister in regard to the free institutions to be extended to the Spanish possessions in the West Indies. Señor Castelar himself publicly stated on another occasion * that, in the question of the abolition of slavery, it was necessary to tolerate the expression, on the part of the United States, of their opinion and of some suggestions, "because this question is one of an international and humanitarian character."

The vacancies in the Cabinet, caused by the resignations of the Ministers of the Colonies and of Finance, were filled by men thoroughly in accord with their colleagues and with the Government majority in the Cortes, and both

* "La Epoca," Madrid, May 4, 1873.

Chambers accepted, by decisive majorities, the proposed colonial policy.

It being advisable that no time be lost, on Christmas Eve the Colonial Minister presented to the Chamber the bill for the immediate emancipation of the slaves in Porto Rico, reading the following royal decree, and the preamble and bill to which it referred :

" In accord with the advice of the Council of Ministers, I hereby authorize the Minister of the Colonies to submit to the deliberation of the Cortes the following bill for the immediate abolition of slavery in the Island of Porto Rico.

" Given in the Palace, the twenty-third day of December, one thousand eight hundred and seventy-two.   AMADEO.

" The Minister of the Colonies

"Tomas Maria Mosquera."

After reading the preamble to the bill, in which it is deplored that the insensate obstinacy of a few rebels does not allow of the granting of the same inestimable boon to Cuba, with the modifications that would necessarily be demanded in view of the different organizations of the system of labor in the two islands, the different density of their population, the enormous inequality in the number of their slaves, and other fundamental differences in their social status: the minister adds that he esteems, as the greatest of his life, the honor he now has in submitting the bill to the consideration of the Cortes.

The Government scheme provided for the total and permanent abolition of slavery in the province of Porto Rico: the slaves to be " de facto" free at the expiration of four months from the date of the publication of the law in the official Gazette of that province. A commission composed of the superior civil Governor of Porto Rico, as chairman, the financial Intendente of the province, the Attorney-general of the audiencia, three persons named by the Provincial Assembly, and three others chosen by the largest slave-owners in the island, was to inquire into the amount of the indemnification for the value of the liberated slaves—such indemnity to be paid within four months of the publication of the law. Of the amount fixed by way of indemnification, eighty per cent. was to be delivered to the owners of the slaves emancipated, half at the charge of the State and the other half at the charge of the province of Porto Rico, the remaining twenty per cent. being at the charge of the owners themselves.

Porto Rico's record was loyal. She had resisted the secession movement of Latin America in 1822, and had fought for Spanish integrity in the war of Santo Domingo. Up to 1837 she had had the same laws and municipal government as the Peninsula. The desire of the island was for the emancipation of her slaves. When consulted in 1866 for the first time as to her needs she ranked first amongst them abolition, and since that period her deputies had continually clamored for it. In this they had been ably seconded by their constituents who, dissatisfied with the incomplete law of 1870, had voluntarily freed many of their slaves. The island was consequently ripe for the radical change contemplated by the present Government, and the dangers attending sudden political or social reforms were reduced to a minimum. Opposition there must necessarily be, for a certain number of planters still clung to the old-fashioned, economical theories, and saw in the liberation of their slaves the ruin of their industrial interests. But it was confidently asserted by the Porto Rican deputies that the proposed measures would encounter but few obstacles, while they would be hailed with enthusiasm by the vast majority. The enthusiasm and determination of the drafters and supporters of the bill, together with its wise and moderate context, made it appear certain that, even in the teeth of the hurricane its discussion raised, it would, at no distant date, become law. Prudent but unscrupulous slave-owners in Porto Rico, in view of the emancipation they had reason to believe at hand, now began shipping their slaves to Cuba, where it was hoped the disturbed political conditions might still long afford a market for their wares. Attention was quickly called to this transportation, and in the Cortes it was denounced as a violation of the laws, an appeal being made for its suppression.

Up to the moment of the introduction of the bill, accompanied by the royal decree, the members of the "league" had cherished the hope that the King would hesitate in giving his support to the Cabinet pledged to the fulfilment of a measure, the very discussion of which had so aroused the country. That the King desired the total abolition of slavery throughout his realm none doubted. But would he dare face the consequences of either failure or success: consequences equally portentous in either event! The " league " contained members of former cabinets; men who had enjoyed the confidence of His Majesty; and these former ministers of the Crown did not hesitate to give countenance to the expectation that the sovereign might still, in the face of the dangerous opposition aroused, pronounce the famous " yo contrario " which, in the preceding June, had cut short the attempted proclamation of martial law throughout the country, and retired Marshal Serrano from office. Knowing Amadeus as they must have known him, their expressed belief, whether feigned or real, as to his action gives us a conclusive proof of the critical nature of the situation. Nor was Amadeus ignorant of its tremendous importance. He knew full well that by his action he must alienate not only immense numbers of former partisans, but incur the bitter enmity of statesmen and conservative leaders who had united with General Prim in establishing his dynasty, and whose defection would place a fearful weapon in the hands of his enemies. Abandoned by those who had been members of his council; . with the prospect of an alliance of his recent supporters with the Carlists in arms in the provinces; and the evidences of disorganization and insubordination in his army, the position of the Sovereign was indeed desperate. Yet in face of the tremendous peril which confronted him, the royal decree of December twenty-third was his answer to Spain and to the world. A great wrong was to be righted, and as far as in his power lay he must aid; the cost of a throne notwithstanding.

Although we cannot but admire the pluck shown by the King, and thoroughly sympathize with the object in view, yet we may question the political wisdom of the step. True, in politics it is not always fair to judge a man, or party, by the result of the action, for rarely does the result correspond with the motive which prompted the action. Yet to the student of this period it is apparent that the existence of slavery in the Spanish dominions was doomed—had been doomed by the principles of the Revolution of 1868— while the constitution of 1869 recognized the equality of all men before the law. The moment selected for the introduction of a discussion of the subject, certain as it was to awake the fiercest passions, was, however, highly inopportune, and was so recognized by the Zorrilla Cabinet in spite of the sympathetic temper of a considerable ministerial majority in the Cortes.

The present writer is inclined to the belief that Amadeus, harassed by the growing instability of his position, and convinced of the improbability of the long continuance of his reign, had determined to force the issue upon friends and foes alike, and to stand or fall on the result. A great opportunity was offered him to accomplish an act of humanity which would receive the sympathy and applause of the civilized world, while circumstances forbade his biding a more favorable political situation. If he failed he must probably sacrifice a crown for which at best he cared but little, and which, under existing circumstances, was a terrible burden. Even with failure the impetus given by his endeavor would eventually—probably at no distant date—carry the question to a satisfactory solution. If this was his reasoning it was correct. The bill which, in its preliminary stages had twice obtained a decisive majority in a monarchical parliament, but which was in serious danger of defeat after the proclamation of the republic, passed the National Assembly on March 22, 1873, by a unanimous vote. Nevertheless History has accorded to

Amadeus the glory of having aimed the death-blow at an institution incompatible with modern morality and the advance of civilization. The abolition of slavery in the West Indies must ever be associated with his name, although his was not the hand which signed the final and definite decree of emancipation.

Before entering upon the description of the last short days of the reign of the Italian prince we may pause to ask ourselves the question, whether Amadeus, with due consistency to the pledges given, could have pursued a different policy on ascending the Spanish throne? Speculation on this head can, of course, be endless, but only profitable while keeping strictly in view the character and disposition of our prince, whereby it is narrowed to but a few legitimate surmises. At the risk of being accused of repetition we must insist on the intensity of qualities, amounting to marked peculiarities in one of Latin origin, namely: Scrupulous observance of the individual rights accorded by the constitution, and reverence for the spirit as well as the letter of the constitution itself. After the proclamation of the republic we shall find the republican orators themselves eulogizing

the late King in their speeches in the Cortes
for this unvarying fidelity, under all circumstances and at all costs, to the pledges given.

Would success have been within his reach
had Amadeus pursued a more vigorously
personal policy from the moment of his advent in Spain? It must be admitted that the
various political parties, although aggressive,
were disorganized and scattered: republicanism was hardly professed: the Carlists
alone were permanently active. On the other
hand, the Treasury was empty; the public
credit well-nigh exhausted; the military and
civil salaries unpaid: in a word the country
on the verge of bankruptcy. By the adoption of energetic measures, by the temporary
exercise of extraordinary powers, many of
these obstacles might have been overcome.
Depleted public coffers have before this been
refilled, and national credit restored, under
auspices as unpromising as those encountered
by the new King. Amadeus himself had
been a witness to the financial and revolutionary straits through which his own country
had passed when Victor Emmanuel was still
only King of Sardinia. But here there existed a wide difference, the importance of
which can hardly be over-estimated. Victor

Emmanuel was of his people : one " of them " in every sense of the word. His responsibilities had come to him by inheritance: by virtue of a long line of ancestors whose interests and history were identical with those of their people ; while Amadeus stood alone : a stranger distrusted and hated by a large portion of his subjects (many indeed subjects in name only). Spain was like a bankrupt joint stock company in the hands of a receiver. Amadeus as the receiver could with strict honesty do no more than reconcile the best interests of the various shareholders with the country's future redemption. The rôle demanded of him was a thankless one necessitating many sacrifices : the reward (doubtful at best) but the tolerance of those he served.

The belief has been expressed in the earlier pages of this study that no ruler of foreign origin, especially one who upheld those provisions of the Revolution of 1868 offensive to the Vatican, could long have preserved his seat on the Spanish throne. Nevertheless the supposition is admissible that, had Amadeus proved a leader, much would have been forgiven him ; while who can say that success, immediate and brilliant military success, might not even have mitigated in the eyes

of the multitude the crime of his alien origin!
Prim was dead, a martyr to political passions
aroused by the advent of the candidate he
had supported. But the astounding physical
courage and the martial bearing of the young
King appealed strongly to a people singularly
influenced by daring, and whose ideals from
time immemorial had been drawn from the
heroes of chivalric romance.

" At least, here is a man ! " had been the
cry of the populace when first they beheld
their young Sovereign.

Success demanded from the outset an iron
hand, and one not over-scrupulous in the
interpretations of personal liberties, or given
to constitutional hair-splitting. But Spain
had taken to herself a King firmly determined
to confine his action strictly to the duties and
obligations he had contracted as a constitutional ruler whose conscientious endeavor
it would be to reconcile by all legitimate
means the conflicting political elements he
found in his path, but who possessed no en-
thusiasms, no illusions. and professed none.
The apparent apathy so often remarked upon
during his short reign arose from two principal causes : overwhelming modesty, not
however to be confounded with timidity, and

deep-rooted distrust of his personal ability to accomplish the task he had reluctantly undertaken. These feelings were never overcome, while to them were soon added disgust at the treachery and falseness displayed by those to whom his confidence was given, followed by lassitude at the futility of all attempts to conciliate the shifting political passions distracting the unhappy country he had been called to govern.

After the abdication Señor Zorrilla asserted from his seat in the Cortes that the monarchy had fallen, *not* by the hands of the republicans or the radicals, but because of the action of those who "demanded, in grave and solemn moments for the country, the suspension of constitutional guarantees."

This would lead us to infer that the mere utterances, at one time or another, of men in his council who advocated stringent measures, not strictly constitutional, had caused his undoing. If this be true how can we doubt that although success might have momentarily crowned such a policy, the result in the long run would inevitably have been the same for his dynasty, while his personal identification with measures ever so slightly at variance with the sacred pledges given might even

have incited a vengeance not unlike that
wreaked on the unfortunate Maximilian in
Mexico.

The opinion of a man such as General
Lanza, at that time Italian Premier, is not to
be lightly set aside, and Lanza considered that
the King had too readily abandoned a situation which even Spanish statesmen of the
opposition did not by any means hold as desperate. But Lanza and the Spanish critics
forgot, or under-estimated the proverbial straw
which may convert the burden silently borne
into the unbearable weight beneath which
the struggling victim must sink. A sneer
here, a slight there : an offensive stare on
this side, a thinly veiled insult on that, are
small things individually—collectively their
import is more serious. Petty annoyances,
it is true, but none the less painful on account
of their smallness and meanness, and especially distressing to the Queen—a particularly
sensitive woman, totally unfitted for the
rough usage never spared those holding conspicuous public positions.

CHAPTER XI.

TURNING in despair from political vexations and humiliations Amadeus found peace and the affection his nature so needed in his family life. In the nursery his sons, Emmanuel and Victor, aged respectively four and three years, were ever-ready play-fellows whose childish pranks he never wearied of, and whose education and amusements we shall find him later personally supervising and sharing.

A dilettante in some respects Amadeus was at the same time a man of intellectual energy and action : physically vigorous he found it incumbent on him to make abundant use of his superfluous vitality. Movement was essential to his nature ; the mental deceptions and worries of his short career on the Spanish throne found their safety-valve in the expenditure of physical force. Mentally Amadeus was said to resemble to a marked degree his grandfather King Charles Albert. Like this ancestor he was a fatalist—like him again he was gifted with an intelligence almost clairvoyant at times in its searching intensity. Prone to distrustful introspection, Amadeus has been charged with vacillation and irresolution, whereas the true cause lay in an abnormal sensitiveness. Unlike his grandfather, however, Amadeus rapidly threw off the moral discouragement occasioned by political discomfiture. He was not morose, but on the contrary was endowed with an almost boyish exuberance of animal spirits, particularly infectious and engaging.

Novara, and his consequent abdication, brought not only mental discouragement but death to Charles Albert; his renunciation of the Spanish throne left Amadeus unconquered, and with mind untrammelled when he assumed more congenial if less exalted duties and responsibilities.

Amadeus never ruled in Spain. It is doubtful whether it was ever intended he should. His mission was that of a pacificator.

Encompassed on all sides by a rigid constitutionalism which left little scope for individual initiative, he must fain be content to guide, in so far as in his power lay, the passions of those responsible before the Nation, without, however, compromising the majesty of his office by permitting himself to be made the tool of party ambition, or intrigue. But it would be a mistake to take it for granted on this account that Amadeus was without a clear and strong personal policy. A free hand was denied him, as much by virtue of his own conscientious scruples as by the constitutional restrictions which bound him.

Maria Victoria was shortly again to become a mother. On this account and by reason of the critical political outlook the holiday functions at Court were this year restricted to the narrowest limit, confined principally to those of a private nature partaken of simply in the family circle. With the advent of the new year, however, the usual deputations must be received, and the customary addresses be patiently listened to and returned.

Although such official addresses are generally very much of the same pattern, consisting of stereotyped eulogistic phrases and well-worn congratulations, those delivered to His

Majesty on January first, 1873, by the deputations of the Senate and House, are, both in view of the existing political situation and the important *dénouement* to follow six weeks later, worthy of reproduction here.

At noon on January first, the King, surrounded by the officers of his household, the Cabinet, Masters of Ceremonies, and high dignitaries of State, stood in the Throne Room of the palace, awaiting the deputations from Parliament. On their entrance the President of the Senate addressed His Majesty as follows:

" Sire: With the opening of the new year, the third year of Your Majesty's reign begins under happy auspices, while the year just closed sees with joy that the work of the constitutional convention, recognized at once by all civilized nations, consolidates itself in a shorter time and fortifies itself with greater strength than institutions and dynasties of traditional origin. The Senate confidently hopes that this third year of Your Majesty's reign will remain fixed among the glories of Spain by the imperishable achievement in humanitarian reform which will soon put an end to slavery in the beautiful province of Porto Rico, notwithstanding the opposition to it by certain egotistical interests and certain political ambitions, against which suffice that firmness of character which distinguishes Your Majesty, and the vigor which the sense of right and the possession of liberty stamp upon the decisions of Congress."

To the above Amadeus replied: "Mr. President: I receive with the highest appreciation and with most profound satisfaction the congratulations which the Senate offers to me to-day, when grateful recollections engage my attention and grave reflections occupy my thoughts; for to-day marks two years since I began to rule in Spain—the commencement of duties in behalf of my new and beloved country, as arduous in their fulfilment as the honor is a high one which I have received at the hands of the Spanish people, by whose will this throne was erected, upon whose love its foundations were laid, and by whose confidence it is to be strengthened and sustained. It is by such means that, while the country enjoys the fruits of the revolution, and while the work of the constituent Cortes is perpetuated, at the same time the energy of popular right manifests itself, in virtue of which new dynasties and modern institutions begin early to take root and acquire for themselves a robust maturity. I accept as a happy omen for the year just now begun the announcement which the Senate makes to me, and the hope the delegates express that those men who now live as slaves in the loyal Spanish province of Porto Rico shall soon enjoy their liberty. A measure so humanitarian and so Christian will be a glory for Spain, an honor for the Cortes, a lustre upon my reign, and a blazon for my dynasty. Civilized nations will find in this a new cause to congratulate themselves upon having recognized from the first moment the work of 1868. Spain will feel a natural pride at seeing herself esteemed and applauded by all the world, while they who have shown themselves distrustful will see that it is not reasonable to fear that an act of justice and humanity may be a source of danger to our prosperity and tranquillity."

The President of the Chamber of Deputies then advanced and read the following words: "Sire: This day, which ushers in a new year in the evolutions of time, recalls to our minds the eve of a solemn moment in the life of Your Majesty, and a memorable epoch in the history of Spanish liberty. The Chamber of Deputies, the immediate representative of the people, lay with joy before the Elect of the Nation the homage of their love, of their respect, and of their unshaken loyalty. Fortunate it is for Spain, and a glory for Your Majesty, that here, in this place, where flattery has so often raised its voice, are to be heard to-day congratulations prompted by the purest affection, and commendations dictated by the most heartfelt sincerity. The Spanish people are now beholding the fulfilment of the hopes with which, two years ago, they greeted Your Majesty for the first time; in your August Person every citizen sees and loves the faithful guardian of popular rights and the swift defender of popular liberties common alike to all Spaniards, without distinction of party or of class. Thus in vain are the plots, the conspiracies, and assaults directed against the popular throne by those who act only in obedience to the baleful influences of party interest; now profaning the sacred name of liberty; now invoking aid from the empty shadows of antiquated institutions, long condemned by history, and now murmuring names which are made more hateful as we are vividly reminded of the intolerable abuses which they symbolize. Reaction, mobocracy, treason itself, if there be in this

loyal land any one capable of treason, shall
be crushed under the weight of public con-
demnation, for Your Majesty, who so well un-
derstands and so wisely practises the sacred
duties of your high office, will ever continue
with unwavering firmness to assist all measures tending towards progress, and to lend
an attentive ear to public opinion, the only
counsellor of democratic sovereigns, and the
only support of thrones founded upon the
free will of a nation. Listening again to
that voice which you have never disregarded,
Your Majesty has now immortalized your
reign by authorizing the presentation of a
bill which, as soon as it shall have been approved by the Cortes and shall become a
law of the realm, will restore the rights of
manhood to the thirty-one thousand unhappy
beings weighed down to-day by the cruelties
of slavery. And if, at the outset, the voice of
disappointed interests, or of hostile opinions,
should cry out against such a sublime act of
humanity, its glorious results shall in the end
allay all ill-will, shall calm every passion,
and shall dispel every apprehension, and (let
Your Majesty doubt it not) our most remote
descendants will bless the hour in which, following the inspirations of right, of justice,

and of public good, you determined to wipe out forever the only blot upon our glorious escutcheon in the eyes of the civilized world. With hopes so well founded and under such happy auspices, the Chamber of Deputies, in the name of the people whom it represents, implores the blessing of Heaven for Your Majesty, for the noble lady whose virtues adorn your throne, and for the royal children who, trained by so pious a mother in the sacred love of liberty, are to-day the hope of the nation, and shall one day be the honor of their family and the just pride of their country."

Before commenting upon this remarkable effusion, we will quote the dignified reply made by His Majesty: " Mr. President: Upon the solemnity of this day, the Chamber of Deputies reminds me that the beginning of my reign corresponds with an epoch memorable for the liberties of Spain. This recollection is to me as proud a one, and as worthy of my regard and appreciation, as is the homage paid to me by your love, your loyalty, and your respect. In guarding and defending public liberties and popular rights, I have only been true to the dictates of my conscience and to the oath which, of my own

free will and in the sight of all the world, I
took in the midst of the Constituent Cortes.
Receiving the assurance, in the name of the
Chamber of Deputies, that the Spanish people
witness the fulfilment of the hopes with
which they greeted me for the first time two
years ago, I feel the greatest pride that a
man may cherish, and the most hearty satisfaction that a monarch may entertain. Full
of the deepest love for this, my adopted country, which, by raising me to the highest dignity, has placed upon me the gravest responsibility, I pray to God that He will grant to
it, in the year which now begins, the peace and
prosperity which it deserves. I am confident,
as is also the Chamber of Deputies, that the
conspiracies directed against liberty and progress will be fruitless in the time to come,
as happily they have been up to the present
moment. And I sincerely and ardently long
for the day when, with all angry passions
laid aside, every one may be persuaded that
there is no opinion and no interest which may
not thrive under the shadow of a throne
founded upon the national will, and daily
more and more identified with the people,
and more firm in its determination to seek
counsel in public opinion, and to give up in

13

the interest of freedom every temptation to injustice and every pretext for violence. The words of approval with which the Chamber of Deputies, the immediate representatives of the people, receives the proposition to abolish slavery in Porto Rico are to me a happy presage that very soon we are to give freedom and happiness to many thousands of men, joy to our Christian hearts, satisfaction to our country, and a just cause of praise to all civilized nations. Profoundly do I thank the Chamber of Deputies for the sentiments expressed toward my wife and my children, whom we shall train up in the love of liberty to the end that they may become worthy of their country."

We may well imagine the smile which played about the King's mouth as he listened to the protestations of the love and affection of his subjects, and the assurances of the happy auspices under which the third year of his reign had begun. Poor Amadeus! The outward and visible signs of the affection of the people, of the loyalty of his advisers, or the support of his adherents, had not been vouchsafed him to any manifest extent during the recent months of political agitation, attempted assassination and vexatious insults.

It was hard to reconcile the ever-increasing difficulties of his position with the flowery optimism of the addresses, and the guarded replies demonstrate the purely official interpretation accorded to utterances prompted by empty etiquette alone. While acknowledging the presages for his dynasty he knew full well that the day when all angry passions would be laid aside could never dawn during his occupancy of the throne.

Some cause for congratulation there certainly was. In the face of the Carlists in arms, " threatened by anarchy and chaos " (the words are Zorrilla's), the Church bill had been presented and passed ; the budget voted, and various minor reforms effected, while the Government had under consideration the reorganization of the police and penitentiary systems, the inauguration of reforms in the criminal laws, and the adoption of other constitutional means to restore and preserve order. But the work accomplished was purely administrative, due largely to the patriotic forbearance of the republican leaders in the Cortes, and the consolidation of the dynasty had become more chimerical as the months rolled by.

In spite of his brave words, Amadeus was

fully aware of the impossibility of a continuance of the actual condition of affairs, and merely awaited the opportunity which would permit of his throwing from his shoulders the burden it no longer profited any one he should bear.

The opportunity was not long in presenting itself. The formation of the anti-emancipation league, with its formidable list of treacherous adherents, and insidious methods to undermine the authority of the Crown, had dealt a staggering blow. This was soon to be followed by one, due, it was asserted, to the machinations of the league, which left the unfortunate sovereign no option but that of abdication or the repudiation of the oath he had taken as constitutional monarch. In such an emergency Amadeus was not the man to hesitate.

The Cortes reassembled on January 15, 1873, and the emancipation act was at once referred to a special committee chosen by the several sections into which the Chamber of Deputies was subdivided for certain legislative purposes. Notwithstanding the general feeling of uneasiness which pervaded political circles, and the unceasing intrigues fomented in all quarters by the league, few anticipated that the climax would so soon be reached. The American diplomat, however, always alert and always well-informed, telegraphed to his government on January 30th that he had reasons to anticipate very soon a change in the form of government, and requested to be instructed as to his line of conduct in case the existing Congress should declare itself a convention and appoint a new Executive.

In the midst of the universal expectancy the royal apartments in the palace were the scene of what, under different circumstances, would have been considered a happy omen. On the night of January 29th the Queen, Maria Victoria, was delivered of a son, to be known later as Prince Louis, Duke of the Abruzzi, and to become a cultivated and efficient officer in the Italian navy.

The official presentation and baptism of the little prince took place in the palace the following day.

Within a fortnight of his entrance into the world this child, who received at his birth the proud titles of Infant of Spain and Prince of the Asturias, was being hurried over the Portuguese frontier in the arms of his mother, who, fainting from

the weakness of fever, and distracted by
anxiety for the safety of her loved ones, was
an exile from the land whose sufferings she
had nobly endeavored to alleviate, and whose
outcasts she had claimed for her especial care
and benefactions.

CHAPTER XII.

WE must now endeavor to describe the
immediate causes which induced the King to
precipitate the step he had long been meditat-
ing.

Some days before the despatch of the telegram to the American Government which
has been quoted, an incident occurred at the
palace, apparently trivial in itself, but which
under existing circumstances, aided by the
skilful manipulations of the League, was des-
tined to prove of sinister import.

During the session of the usual Cabinet
meeting for the transaction of current business, Amadeus had placed before him for

signature the commission appointing a certain General Baltasar Hidalgo to an important command in the northern provinces.

A story was in circulation to the effect that this officer had been implicated in a revolutionary movement which had broken out in the Madrid barracks in 1866, when, a number of artillery sergeants, having gained over their companies, undertook to compel their officers to join them. In spite of this episode, Hidalgo had subsequently held commands both in Cuba and in Spain without exciting comment. On the present occasion, however, it was known that the proposed appointment was unpopular with the General's brother-officers. His Majesty, aware of the objections raised, attempted to dissuade the Minister of War, in view of the discontent which would be caused, from insisting on the appointment. To his surprise he was confronted with a threat of resignation should the promotion be refused. A ministerial crisis at that moment seemed of far more importance than the possible discontent of a few officers of artillery; therefore Amadeus unwillingly yielded to the representations of his Minister and signed the commission.

As soon as it became known that Hidalgo

had received the appointment the entire artillery corps, as an act of protest, tendered their resignations and demanded to be relieved from duty; even those serving before the enemy following their comrades' example, and refusing to recognize the General's authority over any portion of their branch of the service. The resignations of several hundred officers of all grades were thus laid before the Crown.

The situation was serious. Especially so as little doubt could be entertained but that political sympathy with the League, and the knowledge that a large fund had been raised by the same for the maintenance of officers depending on their pay, had influenced many of those who made Hidalgo's appointment the pretext for their resignation. A large majority of the artillery officers stationed in Madrid were known to frequently attend meetings held at the house of Señor Augusto Ulloa, who was in violent and open opposition to the policy of the Zorrilla government.

Once the magnitude of the movement was realized every effort was made to demonstrate the unpatriotic attitude of the corps, whose officers practically deserted in the face of the enemy. But in vain : even those who would have preferred to remain neutral were coerced by their comrades, or by the agents of the Carlists who, on the present occasion, were allied with the League in the plot to undermine the throne.

The desire expressed by General Cordova to resign, recall Hidalgo and himself fill his place was overruled by his colleagues, who were determined on the dissolution of the corps, in spite of the well-known antipathy of the King to sanction such an extreme measure. At the same time all attempts at a compromise were skilfully subverted by those interested in aggravating the political passions on both sides.

The resignations were accepted, and immediate steps taken for the reorganization of the corps. The superior grades were filled by transfers from the engineers and infantry, sergeants being promoted to be company officers.

The impression produced by this lamentable occurrence can well be imagined. Rumors of the wildest nature were spread abroad, while it was asserted that, should the King refuse to undo the acts of the ministry, the other arms would follow the example of the artillery, and that the country would in consequence be left defenceless.

Placed in this unfortunate position, Amadeus was believed to contemplate demanding the resignation of the Cabinet, and making an appeal to the conservatives for aid and support. Time was, however, not allowed the King to put the projects attributed to him into execution. The Cabinet, anticipating difficulties at the palace, adroitly submitted the matter to the Cortes during the memorable session of February seventh, and having obtained a vote of confidence and the approbation of Parliament in their proceedings, presented to the King the decree for the dissolution of the artillery corps under circumstances which left His Majesty no alternative but to sign it.

Tricked by his advisers into following a course which his better judgment condemned, and realizing in the moral and political disorganization of the army, evidenced by the emphatic protest of his officers against an appointment sanctioned by the Crown, the futility of further effort, Amadeus, after signing the second decree, announced to Señor Zorrilla his determination to abdicate the throne.

It was in vain that the Minister, dismayed at the turn the crisis had taken, urged the King to reconsider his resolution. The event had been too long foreseen by His Majesty, and his action on the occasion too carefully weighed to make reconsideration necessary once the step was taken. The utmost Amadeus could concede was an apparent uncertainty, which would allow the Cabinet time to present itself before the Cortes, and, without dangerous precipitation, frame measures for the preservation of order pending the action of the Constituent Assembly on the official announcement of the abdication.

Those about His Majesty were loud in their demands that extreme measures be adopted for the maintenance of the dynasty, and the conservative leaders declared themselves ready to undertake the succession of the Zorrilla Cabinet. Many of those who had heretofore held aloof from the Court were now willing, with the dread of a republic, or worse, before their eyes, to cast in their lot with that of the dynasty they had professed to despise. A deputation of army officers is alleged to have besought His Majesty to authorize them to employ the troops of the Madrid garrison to enable the King to dismiss the Zorrilla

Cabinet, dissolve the Cortes, suspend the constitution, and maintain the throne.

To all these suggestions Amadeus made but one reply; that he had sworn to uphold and obey the constitution; that he had kept his faith with the country, approving all measures sanctioned by the Cortes, and endeavoring to mete out justice equally to all parties. It was now too late for him to give his confidence to those who had kept aloof from the Court until no honorable resource was left but to return his Crown to the Cortes, from whom he had received it, and leave the country free to determine its destinies.

In the words of Collantes, Amadeus abdicated " because he had learned that he had no other supporters than they who were monarchists and partisans of his dynasty only while he gave them power, and who turned against him the moment he changed his Cabinet."

As for the dismissal of the Zorrilla Cabinet and the substitution of a reactionary one, it did not require the eloquence of a Castelar to convince any one that should the King revoke his abdication he could not continue to reign with authority or respect, or form a Ministry which would not immediately find itself in hopeless embarrassment. Jacta alea : once the desire to renounce the Crown formulated, the prestige attached thereto was gone beyond recall. Zorrilla knew this, and he was not the less aware that the King's decision was irrevocable. It is consequently difficult to understand the precise object he had in view while so fervently pleading with His Majesty to delay the official announcement of his renunciation of the throne. It must have been evident to him that the opportunity would immediately be taken advantage of by the republicans. On the other hand, had the King's abdication been solemnly and officially announced to the Cortes, simultaneously with the resignation, *ipso facto*, of the Cabinet, the subsequent discussion by that body as to the necessity of a permanent session, which Señor Zorrilla rightly considered so derogatory to the dignity of a Government still in the exercise of its functions, and which certainly contributed little towards safeguarding the prestige of the Crown, would have been avoided. The result, as far as the action of the Cortes was concerned, which action was duly provided for by the constitution, must have remained the same.

As President of the Council Señor Zorrilla was morally responsible for the crisis forced upon the Crown by the injudicious action of the Minister of War, the consequences of which must have been apparent to a statesman of such vast experience and in a position to be so thoroughly cognizant of the feelings and temper of his countrymen. The accusation of flagrant treachery has, in the humble opinion of the present writer, never been substantiated; at the same time it would seem impossible to absolve the Minister of the committal of a colossal error of judgment, or of being a party to a deliberate attempt to override the legitimate scruples and constitutional prerogatives of his royal master.

Amadeus had communicated his decision to the Prime Minister after the Cabinet council held on Saturday, February 8th. Towards the evening of the following day it began to be noised about that the King had intimated a desire to renounce the Crown, and the matter was eagerly discussed in the theatres and clubs. On Monday morning several newspapers confirmed the report, giving their opinions as to the steps which would be made necessary by such decision. During the course of the day signs of unusual animation

and excitement were visible in the streets and
public places of the capital, and enormous
crowds began to congregate around the palace
of the Cortes. No information had been
vouchsafed, and in consequence the key to
the mysterious situation was loudly demanded
on all sides. The Government had early taken
steps for the maintenance of public order,
but there was no unusual display of force
except in the immediate neighborhood of the
Cortes.

The Cortes met as usual at three o'clock.*
A crowd of deputies filled the lobbies and
committee rooms, but the Chamber itself was
almost deserted, for the members of the Cabinet
had not yet made their appearance, although
it was known that the sitting of the council
was ended, and that the Ministers were actually in the building. The delay caused such
manifest dissatisfaction that Señor Figueras,
the republican parliamentary leader, demanded
of the Chair that the ministers be summoned

---

* In the preparation of the above description of the
occurrences in the Chamber the writer has been
largely indebted to the able and minute report of
General Sickles who, aided by his admirable secretary, Mr. Alvey A. Adee, conscientiously transcribed
the proceedings in detail for the information and
guidance of his Government.

in order that the Chamber might be officially informed of a crisis which it was understood embraced not only the Cabinet, but even the Crown. As Figueras terminated his remarks the Ministers, headed by the President of the council, appeared and took their seats on the Ministrial bench.

Señor Zorrilla at once rose and addressed the House. He said it was true the King had spoken of abdication, but that nothing could transpire officially on so grave a matter until His Majesty had given the subject more reflection. He added that the Cabinet had besought the King to pause in his purpose, and take twenty-four or forty-eight hours to reconsider his determination. In the meanwhile he hoped the House would suspend its sittings, thus leaving the Government disengaged from other duties, so that they might consider and frame the measures most expedient to be brought in for the action of the Cortes.

On the conclusion of the Premier's speech, Señor Figueras again demanded the floor, and insisted on the presentation of a motion that, in view of the serious nature of the crisis, the House should declare itself in permanent session, at the same time professing the fear

14

that, should delay be granted, and the House
be found unprepared, the opportunity might
be seized by the Crown to call the army to
its assistance, thus plunging the nation in
bloodshed.

In vain did Señor Zorrilla disclaim any
official announcement that the King had abdicated, and cling to the statement he made
that Amadeus had spoken of abdication, but
that until the abdication was laid before the
Cortes the dynasty existed and the Ministers
of the Crown were entitled to exercise their
authority. Señor Figueras contended that
once the words had fallen from the lips of
the King, and the President of the Council
had communicated them to the Cortes they
were beyond recall. The political situation
did not permit of the Cortes patiently awaiting till the President informed them that the
King revoked " an irrevocable resolution."
He demanded that there should be no adjourn-
ment; that they should await events in their
seats, and meet them in a way becoming the
magistracy of a great nation. It was necessary that Madrid see a power to protect it:
the Executive had, he considered, ceased to
exist.

Zorrilla replied that the ground taken that

there was now no Executive power confirmed
his position. One of two things must be
done ? If there was an Executive authority,
as he affirmed, there was no need of a permanent Session. If the Chamber thought
that the Executive had ceased to exist, then
let it proceed to name one at once. He
maintained that the Cabinet exercised the
Executive power, with the sanction of the
Crown and the vote of the Chambers, until
dismissed by the one or the other. But
he could not admit that the Government
needed a guardian to see that it performed
its duties.

Señor Martos (Minister of State), having
asked the floor, delivered a long speech, in
which he cleverly combined " compliments
to some, hopes to others, and a mixture of
both for all."

" I said one day, from yonder benches," exclaimed Señor Martos, pointing to the left,
" that when all should be lost, that when unhappily there should be no King, we would
cry : The King is dead—long live the
Nation ! I repeat it now. But let the
Chamber say it when the King is gone. . . .
I am a Minister of the Crown, one of a Cabinet that has thus far merited the confi-

dence of the Chambers.   I must preserve my
honor and loyalty as one of His Majesty's
ministers, and more than ever if His Majesty
persists, in his determination . . . in this
hour of the King's extremity I shall not refuse him my voice, my counsel, or my life.
It is true, gentlemen, that I fear the decision
of the King is irrevocable.   After making
known his purpose I fear he must execute it.
This being so, I ask, can anything be more
clear than the future of the republican party ?
The difficult point in the situation is with
those who are resolved to perform their
duties as a government until the King has
signed his abdication, and until the Cortes
have established such a Government as it may
please them to ordain.   I know that in main-
taining our trust we may see the blood of
the people shed, and you will comprehend
the gravity with which we contemplate the
situation.   This last duty to the dynasty
performed, I am also one of those who will
be found where liberty is fighting, in the
ranks of her common soldiers, indifferent to
the mere name inscribed upon the banner.
This is one of the difficult moments of public
life, not for you, republicans, who have only
to be patient, because, if the King goes, there

is nothing else possible but the republic.
And you, by your impatience, are compromising the republic and liberty! . . . You demand a permanent session. That is to say,
there is no Executive, and the Assembly
assumes all powers. The Government replies
we can preserve order better than an Assembly, because deliberative bodies cannot be
efficient guardians of public order."

Replying to Señor Figueras and the imagi-
nary dangers he had conjured up, the Minister resumed: "Since, then, there is no
occasion for a permanent session. The King
still reigns under the constitution, Ministers
are still at their posts performing their duties,
and the constitution affords the means of
settling all conflicts that may arise. Why,
then, precipitate events? . . . Withdraw
this proposition. Avoid everything not
legal and constitutional in its origin. In
our constitution will be found the remedy
for all our difficulties. Even if chaos comes
and a new creation is necessary, let it appear
with law; let it come from this Chamber if
it is not so born. If our institutions are procured in the streets and from barricades
Liberty is lost. If they come from our
hands, sanctioned by law, we may be sure

their birth will be auspicious, and they will save the country and liberty."

Señor Castelar then rose in his seat, and in one of those matchless outpourings of eloquence for which he stands unsurpassed, pleaded for the permanent session so distasteful to the Cabinet. Warning his colleagues not to expect a speech from him at such a moment, when the display of mere eloquence, the mouthings of a rhetorician, would seem like the levity of Nero strumming the lyre while his capital was in flames, he explains the reality which stares them in the face. " That reality, Gentlemen, is that, without provocation from any one, by the fault of none, the people or the government, the Cortes or any public authority, without a cloud in the sky, the King, the actual King, the elected King, the dynastic King, has announced publicly and solemnly that he hurls from his head to the pavement the Crown of Spain. . . . I ask you, if we concede these twenty-four hours demanded of us, and the King recall his abdication, do you believe he can continue to govern, to reign with authority and respect ? No, never! What Cabinet could he form that we would accept ? What ministry would

not find itself in hopeless embarrassment ?
Who cannot see that in any kind of a republic there would be greater stability than
can henceforth be found in this monarchy ?
. . . You have sought a regal dynasty,
with a patriotic purpose I appreciate, because
you believed the monarchy less subject to
oscillation, less prone to the influence of
popular passions; because you believe that
with a dynasty you could guide the wheel of
fortune; and this monarch of yours, within
a briefer period than the term of a President
of a Republic, without premonition or preparation, like a flash in a clear sky, abandons
you, and you wish now, as a point of etiquette,
that the nation shall sacrifice itself to this
expiring dynasty ! Oh ! my friends ! in
what age, in what nation, let me ask my
eloquent friend the Minister of State, who
is one of the glories of the Spanish tribune,
and who knows history so well, when and
where would etiquette or ceremony, or any
mere form of procedure be preferred to the
public safety ? Do you accept the acts of
our fathers in 1808, when after Ferdinand
the Seventh abandoned the country, they
seized the crown, took away its prerogatives
and privileges, and converted absolute mon-

archy into a constitutional government? Do
you think they should have paused because
the King was absent, because he had abandoned Spain? . . . Can Victor Emmanuel
himself wonder after, confiding to the loyalty
of Señor Zorrilla, and not unworthily, the person of his son, that we hasten to save ourselves
without waiting for forms ; can he complain
when he remembers the treaty he signed with
France—signed it with his own hand—a treaty
vainly invoked at the moment when France,
who had created Italy, found herself in the
depths of an abyss, and when, in defiance to its
provisions, the Italian troops passed the Tiber,
entered Rome, destroyed the most ancient
power known to modern history, and proclaimed on its ruins a constitutional monarchy—and this for the salvation of Italy and
the glory of his crown ? ”

Addressing himself to Señor Zorrilla, the
orator continues:

“ Have I not heard you say in your eloquent speeches that you are indifferent to
the forms of our government? Have you not
always told me the substance was liberty and
democracy? Now, when it is not we who
have destroyed the monarchy, when, in a certain sense and within certain limits, we have

helped you in this last attempt to reconcile monarchy with liberty, will you, while the monarchy falls, will you, like the old rhetoricians and Byzantine disputants, sacrifice liberty at the altar of a fugitive monarchy? It might be otherwise if this Cabinet inspired every one with the confidence I feel in it; if the people knew of it what I know; if all understood its history and pledges to liberty as I recognize them, then none would have fears. But you cannot make nations like individuals; you cannot ignore the agitation that moves Madrid and extends to all the capitals; the distrust that permeates the country; the currents that may impel us to a fearful catastrophe. Let me plead with you; let me pray you, not as a deputy of the minority, but as a Spaniard, to avoid this peril by an immediate decision, now, while you can yet save the person of the King, although you cannot save his authority, or his crown. . . . Let us, then, accept the proposition to go into permanent Session. You ask for twenty-four hours! The King asks this delay, through the President of the Council. We do not ignore the King. He has ignored himself: we ignore nothing, absolutely nothing. We, the depositaries of the national sovereignty, choose to exercise a power never denied, not even by the ancient monarchs to the Cortes, a supervisory power that does not permit us to cease our vigilance over the public welfare. What right has the Cabinet or the fugitive monarchy to object to the performance of this duty ? . . ."

On the conclusion of Señor Castelar's stirring appeal Zorrilla again asked the attention of the House. He wished, he said, to elucidate a situation which was evidently misunderstood. The republican speakers affirmed that the country was without a King or a dynasty. This was not true. There was evidently a desire to precipitate events and to alarm the Chamber. The proposition of Señor Figueras was disrespectful to the Cabinet and the Government ; his explanations as well as Señor Castelar's remarks, had given it a special signification. A permanent session was desired in order that, should the King reconsider his decision, he may be confronted with the assertion that it was too late ; and if he persisted that his renunciation may be accepted. " A permanent session," argued the Minister, " if granted, can have no other object than the one I have indicated. It is designed in this permanent session to vote a guardian for us that we have not asked. You are about to say that you have no confidence in us. (Cries of No, No!) Yes—because half-way confidence is no confidence. Having said this, do as you please; but bear in mind that if the King has taken forty-eight hours to consider and decide, he has done so at the solicitation of the Council of Ministers. Let each one choose his side, which we will not discuss now, for to-morrow history will do justice to all. The Government has brought nothing official here for debate or action. The Government does not consent that the Chamber shall declare itself in permanent session. The Government, in so far as it is not derogatory to its dignity, nor menacing to responsible power, would have no objection to the adoption of a proposition. But the republican minority, not satisfied with this, demands a permanent session for the purposes I have indicated. I am responsible for order and liberty. When the present emergency is over, whatever may be the solution adopted, I shall retire to some obscure corner. I do not wish to weary the Chamber. If the solution we approach contributes to the happiness of the country all of us will rejoice. for we have only sought the public prosperity. If, on the contrary,

an unfortunate result is in store for us let us
not hasten the catastrophe, but rather await
quietly that dread reality which I fear must
be, when that institution which we believe
was the best guarantee of the most perfect
order and the most absolute liberty shall have
disappeared."

Señor Castelar again insisted that the proposition did not imply distrust of the Government, that, on the contrary, it was a measure
of precaution to strengthen its hands in the
critical moments they were traversing. The
President of the council had accused them of
wishing to forestall the reconsideration of
the King ; but what idea had His Excellency
of the dignity and firmness of the Monarch!
The King could not recall his resolution, and
consequently the Cortes could not occupy
itself with his reflections, or sacrifice the
welfare of the country to personal questions.

Señor Figueras expressed the same sentiments. He added that he did not insist that
the Cabinet should remain in the Chamber ;
nor was it necessary that those deputies who
did not share his apprehensions should remain there. He did not propose any deliberation ; they would remain without action,
but organized and ready for action. Should

his proposition be refused he predicted days of bloodshed and mourning for Madrid, the responsibility of which would be on the heads of those who so obstinately refused so just a remedy.

A pause followed and it became apparent that the Cabinet was not of one mind as to the course to be pursued. Zorrilla and Martos disagreed as to the expediency of yielding to the demand for a permanent session, and the latter was about to leave the ministerial bench but was dissuaded from so doing by his colleagues, and reluctantly resumed his seat. Whereupon Señor Zorrilla arose, and repelling all efforts to detain him abruptly left the Chamber.

Señor Martos again requested Señor Figueras to explain the exact nature of his proposition, which the republican deputy proceeded to do in very nearly the same words which have been above quoted.

"Señor Figueras desires that, without action, we remain assembled here, prepared for any contingency, the flag flying over the palace as the sign that the Chamber is in session!" petulantly exclaimed the Minister. "Well, then, would to God that with the same facility we might settle the difficulties of to-day and those that may come to-morrow."

Congress immediately ordered a permanent session without deliberation, the presiding officers to remain in the Chamber attended by a special committee appointed for the purpose.

At nine o'clock the session was suspended " pro forma " after a sitting of six hours' duration.

CHAPTER XIII.

DURING the course of the afternoon and evening the principal thoroughfares of the capital became densely thronged with the multitudes eagerly awaiting news of the action of the Cortes.

The Puerta del Sol, the true forum of Madrid, the centre of popular agitation or gossip, was a seething mass of human beings. In the cafés, from the balconies, from the parapet of the great fountain in the square, improvised politicians harangued little knots of sympathizers or those drawn merely by curiosity to the accepted meeting-place. The tension was extreme, for although it was very generally admitted that the debate in the Cortes could have but one result, opinions varied as

to the means which would be employed for
the establishment of the Republic, while excitement was kept at the highest pitch by a
feeling of uncertainty as to the possible action of those still nominally in power at the
Royal Palace. Nor were those idle who from
selfish motives maliciously circulated rumors
of the King's decision to revoke his abdication, and, if necessary, employ force to vindi-
cate the prerogatives of his dynasty. To
these the rabble lent a not unwilling ear,
scenting in the prospect of strife and disorder
opportunities denied them alike by monarchical or republican institutions.

In the immediate neighborhood of the Palace of the Cortes the multitude was most compact, and consisted largely of those who took
a more intelligent interest in the proceedings
of the legislative body assembled within its
walls. To these republican deputies showed
themselves at intervals from the windows and
balconies, giving out scraps of information of
the tenor and progress of the debate going
on within. The leaders issued a printed
address which was posted in all parts of the
city, assuring their partisans of a prompt and
peaceful republican solution of the crisis, and
exhorting the populace to remain calm ; urg-

ing the necessity of avoidance of all unlawful demonstrations. While the Government had made known to the military and civil authorities throughout the Kingdom the probable abdication of the Sovereign, and urged that all possible measures and precautions for the maintenance of order be adopted, the republican leaders had taken care to advise their friends and adherents in the provinces of the favorable aspect of affairs for their cause, imitating the Government in their exhortations for the observance of patience and calm.

The Royal Palace was enveloped in gloom, although a continual stream of ministers, statesmen and military and civil dignitaries, flowed through its huge portals. The King was busily occupied in the preparation of the Message by which he was to make known to the Cortes on the morrow his formal abdication of the throne on which they had placed him. In the private apartments, in spite of the Queen's illness, preparations were rapidly being made for departure, it having been decided that the King and royal family should start at the earliest possible moment for Lisbon, where Amadeus' younger sister, Queen Maria Pia, offered a warm hospitality.

15

The Government, without making any untimely display of military force, had provided amply for the preservation of the King's person, as well as that of the palace, from any possible attack by a misguided mob. Detachments of the citizen-militia guarded the various public buildings, and occupied the most thickly crowded quarters. The main body of the garrison was, however, kept in barracks although under arms. In spite of the general tension the hours of the night passed, and the dawn of the eventful eleventh of February broke without the public tranquillity having been seriously disturbed.

On suspending the sitting the night before the President had convoked the Chamber at three o'clock on the following day. At the appointed hour, on Tuesday, February eleventh, Señor Rivero called the House to order, and stated that the following communication had been received from the Government:

"To the President of the Chamber of
    Deputies:

"Your Excellency: At half-past one this afternoon, accompanied by the Minister of State, I presented myself in the royal chambers, in compliance with His Majesty's request, and received from the King the inclosed document, which I have the honor to transmit to Your Excellency, in order that it may be communicated to Congress."

(Signed)   " MANUEL RUIZ ZORRILLA.
" MADRID,
" February 11, 1873."

Amidst respectful silence, in an atmosphere of intense suppressed emotion, the secretary read the abdication of the King, couched in the following words :

" TO THE CHAMBER :

" Great was the honor bestowed upon me by the Spanish nation when it elected me to occupy its throne, an honor all the more appreciated by me since it was offered to me environed by the difficulties and dangers which accompany the task of governing a country so deeply agitated.

" Animated, however, by the firmness of purpose natural to my race, which seeks rather than shuns danger; fully determined to seek my sole inspiration in the good of the country, and to raise myself above all party level; resolved to fulfil religiously the oath I took before the Constituent Cortes; and ready to make all manner of sacrifices in order to give to this heroic nation the peace it needs, the freedom it deserves, and the greatness to which its glorious history and the uprightness and constancy of its sons entitle it, I thought that my limited experience in the art of governing would be compensated for by the loyalty of my nature, and that I should find powerful aid in warding off the dangers and conquering the difficulties, that were not hidden from my view, in the sympathy of all those Spaniards who, loving their native land, were desirous of putting an end to the bloody and barren struggles which for so many years have been gnawing at its vitals.

"I realize that my good intentions have been in vain.   For two long years have I worn the Crown of Spain, and Spain still lives in continual strife, departing day by day more widely from that era of peace and prosperity for which I have so ardently yearned.   Had the enemies to her happiness been foreigners, then, at the head of our valiant and tried soldiers, I would have been the first to give them battle.   But all those who, with sword and pen and speech, aggravate and perpetuate the troubles of the nation, are Spaniards;

they all invoke the hallowed name of country ; they all strive and labor for its well-being ; and, amidst the din of combat, amidst the confused, appalling, and contradictory clamor of the contestants, amidst so many and so widely opposed manifestations of public opinion it is impossible to choose the right, and still more impossible to find a remedy for such vast evils. I have earnestly sought a remedy within the bounds of law. Beyond this limit he who is pledged to obey the law has no right to go.

" None will attribute my determination to weakness of spirit. No danger could move me to take off the Crown from my brow if I believed that I wore it for my country's good. Neither have I been influenced by the peril that threatened the life of my august wife who, in this solemn moment, joins me in the earnest hope that in good time free pardon may be given to the authors of that attempt.

" Nevertheless, I am to-day firmly convinced of the barrenness of my efforts and the impossibility of realizing my aims.

" These, Deputies, are the reasons that move me to give back to the Nation, and in its name to you, the Crown offered to me by the national suffrage, renouncing it for myself, my children, and my successors.

"Be assured that, in relinquishing the Crown, I do not give up my love for this noble and unhappy Spain, and that I bear away with me from hence no other sorrow than that it has not been possible for me to accomplish for her all the good my loyal heart so earnestly desired.

(Signed) " AMADEUS.

" PALACE OF MADRID,
    " February 11, 1873."

An impressive silence followed the reading of the King's farewell words to the nation he had so honestly endeavored to serve. Then slowly rising to his feet the President addressed the House:

" Gentlemen of the Chamber: the renunciation of the Crown of Spain by Don Amadeo, of Savoy, remands to the Spanish Cortes the sovereign authority over the Kingdom. This event would be grave if, in the presence of the majesty of the Cortes, anything could be grave or difficult. As this Chamber cannot, by itself, exercise the powers now devolved on Congress, the presence and co-operation of the Senate being necessary, I have the honor to propose that a message be addressed to that body, which is already prepared, in order that both Chambers, representing the sovereign authority, shall take such action in relation to the document just read as the emergency demands."

This motion having been agreed to without debate, a brief recess was taken, pending the arrival of the reply from the Senate; which was, however, not long delayed. Its contents stated that the Senate considered it necessary that the two Houses should meet as one Assembly to provide for the public safety. A few moments after the receipt of this message, the members of the Senate, preceded by two mace-bearers, entered the Chamber. The President of the Senate occupied a seat to the right of the President of the Chamber, who acted as presiding officer of the Sovereign Cortes: the senators seated themselves promiscuously among their colleagues of the House. Secretaries on behalf of both Houses having been selected, the President declared that the Sovereign Cortes of Spain were organized and in session, and ordered the King's act of abdication to be read again.

On the conclusion of the second reading Señor Martos, Secretary of State, spoke as follows: " The President of the Council of Ministers is unable to present himself before the Chambers in these grave, and for us most unhappy circumstances, to address the Sovereign Cortes of Spain. In endeavoring, as far as I can, to fill his place, I have a few words to address you. Neither the weight of responsibility pressing upon me, nor the solemnity of the situation surrounding us permits anything like a speech from me at this moment. The occasion demands of us prudent, salutary and great acts. I have only to say to you, Gentlemen, that His Majesty the King of Spain, Don Amadeo I. of Savoy, to whom we still hold the relation of responsible advisers, has announced to us this morning his irrevocable resolution to resign the Crown into the hands of the Sovereign Cortes, the representatives of Spain, from whom he received it. In view of this impressive circumstance, it is needless for me to advert to the obvious responsibilities and duties devolving upon this Assembly, duties which it cannot fail to comprehend and fulfil. With this communication, Gentlemen, the powers of the present Government cease.

In the name of my colleagues, on their behalf
and for myself, I now surrender the powers we
received from the King to this Assembly,
which from this moment becomes the sole
and only sovereignty. May Almighty God
grant to all of us the wisdom of which the
country has need! May all Spaniards unite
with us, as the country may rightfully demand of them, for the salvation of liberty and
the guardianship of the interests of society."

The members of the Cabinet then left the
ministerial bench and took their seats among
the deputies.

Another pause followed. The voice of the
President clearly enunciated: "Do the Sov-
ereign Cortes accept the resignation of the
Crown tendered by Don Amadeo of Savoy?"

The resignation was accepted without a
dissenting voice.

"Do the Cortes," again queried the President, "agree to send a message to this illustrious Prince, expressing their regret and accepting the resignation?"

This also was agreed to unanimously, as was
the formation of a committee to draft and
report a message. On the committee figured
the names of Castelar, Figueras, Rivero, the

Marquis of Sardoal, and others. When the committee returned to the Chamber bringing with them the report they had prepared, Señor Castelar requested that he might be allowed a word of explanation before the message was read. Naturally, he said, the members of the committee were not agreed upon the terms in which the address to the King should be couched. But they understood it was not a moment to insist upon personal or party sentiments. It was believed the message was a faithful expression of the views of the majority of the Sovereign Cortes.

Señor Castelar then himself read the message.

"THE NATIONAL ASSEMBLY TO HIS MAJESTY DON AMADEO I.

"Sire: The Sovereign Cortes of the Spanish Nation have heard with solemn respect the eloquent message of Your Majesty, in whose chivalrous words of uprightness, of honor, and of loyalty they have seen fresh witness borne to the high endowments of intelligence and character that distinguish Your Majesty, and of the exalted love you bear to this your second country, which, generous and brave, cherishing its dignity even to superstition, and its independence even to heroism, can never, never forget that Your Majesty has been the head of the State, the personification of its sovereignty, and the chief authority within the sphere of its laws ; nor can it fail to discern that, in offering honor and praise to Your Majesty, it honors and ennobles itself.

" Sire : The Cortes have been faithful to the commands of their constituents, and guardians of the institutions they found already established by the will of the nation in the Constitutional Assembly. In all their acts and decisions the Cortes have restrained themselves within the bounds of their prerogatives, and have respected the will of Your Majesty and the rights belonging to Your Majesty under our constitution. While proclaiming this loudly and clearly, in order that upon them may never fall the responsibility of this issue, which we accept with regret, but which we shall meet with energy, the Cortes unanimously declare that Your Majesty has been a faithful, a most faithful, observer of the respect due to these Chambers, and that you have faithfully, most faithfully, kept the oath made when Your Majesty ac-

cepted from the hands of the people the
Crown of Spain: a glorious, a most glorious,
record, in this age of ambitious and dictatorial
sway, when, seated on the inaccessible
heights of a throne, which only a few privi-
leged ones ascend, the least adventurous of
rulers have not restrained their ambition for
absolute authority.

" Your Majesty may justly say, in the privacy of your retirement, in the bosom of your
lovely land, and by the fireside of your
family, that if any human being could have
checked the irresistible course of events, Your
Majesty, with your constitutional education
and your respect for established law, would
have done so, absolutely and completely.
Convinced of the truth of this, the Cortes,
had it been in their power, would have made
the utmost sacrifices to induce Your Majesty
to desist from your purpose, and to recall your
renunciation,

" But, knowing as they do the unswerving character of Your Majesty, justice to the
maturity of your ideas, and the firmness of
your purpose, prevents the Cortes from pray-
ing Your Majesty to reconsider your determination, and decides them to announce that
they have assumed the Supreme Power and

Sovereignty of the Nation, in order that, under such critical circumstances, and with the promptness demanded by the gravity of the peril and the transcendency of the situation, they may minister to the salvation of democracy—the base of our political structure of liberty—the soul of all our rights and of the country—our immortal and loving mother, for whom we are all resolved to freely sacrifice not only our individual ideas but also our name and our very existence.

"Our fathers battled with even more adverse circumstances at the beginning of this century, and, inspired by these ideas and these sentiments, it was given them to conquer. Abandoned by their King, their native soil overrun by foreign hosts, and menaced by that giant mind that seemed to possess the talisman of destruction and of war, the Cortes driven to an island at the furthermost verge of the country, not only saved their fatherland and wrote the glorious epic of its independence, but, upon the wide-scattered ruins of the old social structure, they laid the foundation of the new. The Cortes feel that the Spanish Nation has not degenerated, and they trust that they themselves will still less degenerate from the austere and patriotic virtues that distinguished the founders of liberty in Spain.

When all dangers shall have been warded off, and all obstacles overcome ; when we shall have emerged from the difficulties that attend every epoch of transition and of crisis, the Spanish people—which, while Your Majesty remains upon our noble soil, will offer you every mark of respect, of loyalty, and of deference, because it is due alike to Your Majesty, to your virtuous and noble Consort, and to your innocent children—-the Spanish people cannot offer you a Crown in the future, but they will then offer you another dignity, —the dignity of a citizen in the midst of a free and independent people.

PALACE OF THE CORTES,
    February 11, 1873.

It does not require great perspicuity to trace the eloquence of Castelar in the rounded and high-sounding sentences of the address. Nor can we wonder that, when declaimed with the dramatic force of that incomparable orator, its deliverance was frequently interrupted by " loud applause from all parts of the Chamber." With such a guarantee for good conduct in his pocket, Amadeus might aspire to the suffrages of any throne which happened to be vacant : unless, indeed, he preferred "the dignity of a citizen in the midst of a free and independent people." This dignity he did prefer—but amidst a nation whose ideas of freedom and independence differed materially from those entertained by their Spanish cousins, and of the sincerity of whose affection he was more convinced : in the bosom of his own beloved Italy.

In addition to appointing a committee to present the address to His Majesty, the Cortes proceeded to nominate another whose duty it should be to accompany the ex-monarch to the Spanish frontier. These formalities accomplished, President Rivero resumed the chair,—and announced that a proposition was in his hands to be submitted to the Chamber.

"We are approaching a solemn moment in the national history ; " urged Señor Rivero. "I count upon your calmness, dignity and prudence, since these are the virtues of Sovereignty."

The proposition, signed by seven of the most influential republican names, asked Congress to approve that the National Assembly, assuming all power, declare that the form of

government of the nation be republican, re-
mitting to a Constituent Convention the organization of this form of government ; and
further that the Assembly choose an Executive, removable by and responsible to the
Chamber.

CHAPTER XIV.

ALTHOUGH convinced of the present necessity for a republican form of government, a large number of the deputies who would shortly be called upon to cast their vote in favor of this system were determined to do so on purely patriotic grounds, thereby making their political creed subservient to the immediate exigencies demanded by the critical situation of their country.

That a serious conflict must result between the party of progress, rallying under the republican flag, and the reaction symbolized in the person of the young Prince Alfonso, son of Queen Isabella, had been anticipated by those who watched the gradual decline of

16   241

the star of the Savoy dynasty. But it had also been foreseen, and duly admitted that, reinforced as the republicans would be by the adhesion of influential men, not heretofore acting with that party, a temporary triumph of the republican principles must result. In other words, many monarchists were inclined to look upon the Republic as the means and not the end of their dynastic aspiration. Time has proved these political forecasts to have been well founded. Again many of those who served the Savoy dynasty were at heart republican in their sympathies. A close observer, and one who appreciated the subtle distinctions of the Spanish politics of the early seventies, has said that, between Rivero, Martos and Becerra on the one hand, and Castelar, Figueras and Pi y Margall on the other, the line of demarcation was rather one of party association than of ideas or ulterior purposes. They were all republicans, the former making a détour by a path that was soon to intersect the straight road taken by the latter. Collantes recognized the necessity of a republican interregnum ; but he did not abandon his allegiance to the Bourbon dynasty when he assured the republicans that he would neither stint his applause nor refuse his sympathy if the country was happy and prosperous under their régime. The policy he advocated to his friends was to patiently await their own triumph.

" The radicals have given success to the republicans ; " he exclaimed. " Who knows but that the republicans may give it to us ! "

His party made no more pretence of sympathy with the republicans than they had for Amadeus, yet they would place no obstacles in the way, should such doctrines be proved compatible with the national interests. In recognition of this forbearance he asked that the republicans should remember the conduct of his party to-day that they might follow it to-morrow, should they in turn fail in their undertaking.

In view of the wide divergence of creed held by those taking leading parts in it, the debate was to prove of peculiar interest. Without a link of real sympathy, but drawn together by the common danger which threatened their country, those thus temporarily united, while prepared to accept the republican solution imposed upon them by the abnormal condition of affairs, yet held themselves free to assert their own political convictions at such time as they might deem opportune. The patriotic forbearance of those who made the temporary sacrifice of their personal and party convictions, in order to save their country from the horrors of revolution and bloodshed, is worthy of the highest commendation. It is doubtful, however, if even the most enthusiastic republican leaders were really deceived as to the probable stability of the system they were so anxious to inaugurate.

Before the debate was declared open Señor Pi y Margall requested permission to say a few words in explanation and support of the proposition he had signed. The ministers who had received their authority from the hands of the King had, he argued, disappeared with the authority of the person from whom they derived their trust. But one legitmate source of authority remained—the Cortes. If the Cortes hold the Legislative Power they must create an Executive. He proposed that this be chosen by a direct vote of the Assembly, and that it be charged with the duty of enforcing the decrees issued by the Cortes. A return to monarchical principles was impossible after such repeated failure. A constitutional monarchy had been established in the person of a Queen by divine right—yet it could not be reconciled with liberty, and the Queen was banished. An attempt was then made to establish an elective monarchy and a King impersonating it was chosen. This Sovereign now confessed himself unable to overcome the rancor of parties, or the discord devastating the country. Dissensions had multiplied: animosities had spread and extended even to the parties that made the revolution of September, 1868. Those who had established the great principle of national sovereignty in the people, could not do less than accept a form of government compatible with this principle ; and this could not be found in a monarchy which circumscribes the power in the hands of a single family. What was needed were movable powers: the Executive should be so constituted that it be ever in harmony with the ideas of the Spanish people, and this the Republic alone could accomplish. He and his party considered that this should take the form of a federation, but for the present he would be satisfied with the proclamation of a Republic, leaving to a Constitutional Convention, to be chosen later, the duty of defining the organization and form of the Republic.

The debate having been declared open, Señor Romeo Ortiz, speaking on behalf of his party, stated, that although it could not be expected of those who were monarchists by conviction, that they should abandon their ideas and suddenly turn republicans, still they were nevertheless disposed to lend loyal and sincere support to the power that might be created to preserve public order, and maintain the integrity of the territory.

A discussion then arose between the President and Señor Zorrilla, which latter maintained that since the resignation of the late Cabinet considerable peril threatened them as there was no one now responsible for public safety, or in a position to issue instructions to military or civil functionaries in the provinces.

Señor Rivero contended that after the late ministry resigned their powers into the hands of the Assembly, that body exercised them. In his opinion, when the Sovereign Assembly undertook the functions of government, his own authority as President should be sufficient until another was named. But he considered that he had a right to call upon the retiring ministers to assist him in the preservation of order until their successors were named. Should disturbances arise in Madrid or the provinces, he would rely upon the ministers to suppress them during the short period in which their assistance would be necessary. In order not to delay the progress of the debate he proposed that the late Cabinet resume their seats on the ministerial bench, exercising Executive functions until the Assembly name their successors.

This proposition was approved by the Chamber, but Señores Zorrilla and Martos at once sprang to their feet in vigorous protest. They were, however, called to order, and again requested, in the name of the country and of the National Assembly, to take their places on the ministerial bench, and discharge the functions of their separate offices. Further signs of protest being apparent the President declared that the question was not debatable, and, in the name of the Assembly, and to support its authority, insisted that the late Ministers obey. This led to an outburst of indignation. Zorrilla stoutly maintained that he had resigned; Martos demanded the right to speak from his seat as a deputy ; Las Cuevas accused the President of assuming a dictatorship; while Figueras clamored for the Assembly to confine its discussion to the choice

of a Government. In the confusion Señor
Rivero attempted to defend his position, but
with difficulty succeeded in making himself
understood to the effect that he had relied on
the patriotism of the late Cabinet to discharge
its function until the appointment of its successor.

Martos continued to demand the floor,
which was finally ceded him. He claimed
that in the discussion he had only insisted
on his right as a deputy, which had at last
been conceded to him after an undue resistance that might have been wisely avoided.
He regretted that tyranny should begin the
very day the monarchy disappeared.

At these words, in spite of the protests
and efforts to detain him, President Rivero
sprang from his seat and, confiding the Chair
to Señor Figuerola, President of the Senate,
abruptly left the Chamber.

Señor Martos then proceeded to explain
more calmly the position of the late Cabinet
which, he said, was incapable of declining any
responsibility, above all under such difficult
circumstances. But they could not accede
to the imperious demand made upon them.
His own right as a deputy had been attacked,
and he had simply defended it. The King's

authority having ceased by reason of his abdication, their resignations had been given to the Cortes, the sovereignty of which Assembly they recognized. Had the request for them to reassume their functions been made in a different tone, they might have yielded to the desire and vote of the Sovereign Assembly. Señor Martos stated further that the executive duties springing out of the present situation devolved upon the Presidency of the Cortes, resting at the same time upon each and every member of that body. For the maintenance of public order means were at the disposition of the representative of the Cortes, or of whomsoever might be charged with the exercise of its powers. In conclusion, he begged to be allowed to withdraw the harsh expressions he had uttered in defence of his rights as a deputy.

To the appeal from President Figuerola, who stated that he recognized the motives of delicacy which caused the members of the retiring Cabinet to hesitate to resume their functions, and the inability of the Assembly to oblige them to do so, but who at the same time urged them to lay aside all questions of form, and, by taking their places on the ministerial bench, provide the necessary safeguards for public order, Señor Martos replied that this course was not necessary. The public business, he added, was being transacted through the under-secretaries of the various departments, while General Cordova, not as Minister, but as General of the army and as a patriot, was present in the Ministry of War, guarding the interests confided to its charge.

These explanations having given satisfaction, the late Minister stated that the Cabinet would prefer not to occupy the ministerial bench, because of the important measures about to be adopted, in the debate concerning which the members desired to take part in their capacity as deputies. The incident being declared terminated the discussion was resumed on the main proposition.

The leaders of various parties now claimed permission to qualify the votes they would shortly cast.

The Marquis de Bazzanallana, of the Senate, said that they were asked to vote a form of government he and his friends had never believed in : to assist in establishing a Republic. But they would bow their heads before the current of events, and overlook irregularities to which they had in no manner contributed.

Inspired only by sentiments of patriotism, they offered their co-operation to the end that the government which was to be established should be strong, and have the necessary means to assure order and peace to their unfortunate country. During the century the republic was the only form of government not yet tried in Spain. God grant that the republican party be proved to include in its ranks not only great orators but also great statesmen!

The speaker was followed by the young Marquis de Sardoal, who had already made his mark as an able and brilliant debater, and who rose to explain the meaning of the votes his friends would give.

" You will understand, " he said, " that having been monarchists yesterday, we continue to be so to-day; that those of us who have heretofore believed liberty compatible with monarchy do not admit that the accident of the abdication of the late King has affected the principle which constitutes the foundation of our opinions. We cannot say to those who have always been republicans that our monarchical faith is impaired. Such a declaration would justify your suspicions, and we desire to retain your respect. The situation is difficult, the country and social order are menaced and impel us to action; we shall yield to the exigency, as far as our dignity permits, because we hold above our opinions and antecedents the welfare of Spain. Comprehending that the monarchy we have defended is now impossible; comprehending that monarchy is not an abstraction and can only be realized in the establishment of a dynasty, and this being here, and now, impracticable, we vote the Republic. . . . We are not among those who will pretend to march with your leaders. We shall be with you as soldiers in the ranks, uniting with you in the love of country and of liberty and social order. Our vote has still another aspect. Foregoing forms which, under other circumstances, we might deem indispensable, we recognize the imperative necessity of depositing the Government, now abandoned, in some hands, and, therefore, we shall vote the Republic; but with the understanding that your power will not extend beyond the moment when the Constitutional Convention that will be elected shall have met and shall have determined the form of government to be permanently founded. . . ."

The speaker believed the course taken by his party to be honorable, yielding as they did, for the present, their opinions to the general welfare of the country and the consolidation of its liberties.

Señor Martos considered that they were all giving an example unparalleled in history: without violence, without tumult, without the effusion of blood, without external pressure, a free vote would be taken, uninfluenced by a single act of force. What the Marquis de Sardoal had said for himself and some of his friends might have been declared in the name of the whole radical party: they certainly had not desired the events they were witnessing and which they bitterly deplored: believing as they did in the salvation of liberty with the Savoy dynasty, they were undergoing no sudden transformation of opinions. They had taken no initiative in proposing the republic: it was the right of the professed republicans to take such initiative. "I rejoice," he exclaimed, "that the republican party receives us, and I rejoice in this above all for the sake of the country and of liberty. But let it be understood that, in contributing to your ends, we have only consulted our duty. I respect all opinions, as I desire that mine may be respected. I say, without taking an initiative in the proposition under discussion, that we accept it and shall vote it. The republic will be order and peace. And herein we are united—the republicans of yesterday and the monarchists of to-day are all republicans from to-morrow, to save democracy, liberty, and all the interests of society." Señor Zorrilla again claimed the attention of his colleagues, and gave his reasons for declining to occupy his seat on the Government bench. He could not accept the republic, he stated, although all his sympathies were with those on the side of liberty. This would see the end of his political career; once before he had desired to end it, but had been persuaded against his will to return to public life. No one could appreciate what he had suffered during the last eight days. Now that he was about to retire into private life, he wished to conclude by defining his position. " I believe," he began, "that he who, as President of the Constituent Cortes, most of all influenced the establishment of the Monarchy; that he who went to Italy to offer the Crown to the Duke of Aosta; that he who has been Minister of the King, and twice President of the Council of Ministers; that he who has given the pledges that I have given, and who is placed in the situation in which I find myself; that he who cherishes the personal regard that I have professed for the late King —and my colleagues know it well—for they know that I have supported the dynasty and monarchy in the Tertulia Club, and that I have been a liberal and radical in the palace; he who has been thus placed, and who now finds himself here, and who after all this has no faith, as I have had none for a year or more, neither in parties nor in men, could have no motive under existing circumstances for remaining in public life unless he believed he could in some manner contribute to the triumph and consolidation of liberty. I retire, then, Gentlemen, to private life; but I cannot do less than add a few more words, for one cannot abandon in a moment the inclinations and the feelings of a lifetime. My party elected me its chief, and those of them who are here, and those who are elsewhere, are at liberty to adopt any opinions they find agreeable. As to the situation of my country, I wish to record that the only way in which republicans and monarchists could have allied liberty and order was to have supported resolutely, each within their sphere, the dynasty of Savoy. At the same time I wish it to be recorded that neither the liberals nor the republicans have overthrown the dynasty. When it was proposed to suspend the constitution upon the allegation that anarchy menaced the country, I could not comprehend how that Government could have wished these guarantees suspended, when precisely those who provoked the anarchy were the advocates of the measure. I do not make allusions to anybody. I conclude: I am a monarchical partisan of the dynasty of King Amadeus, of Savoy. I have been his President of the Council of Ministers—and I do not recognize my right to be anything else. I desire good fortune and happiness for those who are here charged with the duty of guarding liberty. All the world knows where my sympathies go, and I need not affirm them. I have done."

After a ringing speech from Señor Collantes, quotations from which have already been given above, and a short passage of arms (frequently interrupted by impatient cries for a vote) between Señores Zorrilla and Ulloa, the latter having taken exception to

the insinuation that his party was responsible
for the fall of the late dynasty ; Señor Castelar
craved the indulgence of the Chamber.
" Gentlemen," he cried, " The republican
party does not claim the glory that might
belong to it of having destroyed the Monarchy.
Nor can we permit you to throw upon us the
responsibility of this grave situation. No ;
nobody has destroyed the Monarchy in Spain ;
nobody has killed it ! In contributing to
improve the opportunity before us I cannot
in my conscience claim any merit in destroying the Monarchy. The Monarchy died by
internal decomposition. The Monarchy dies
without any one having contributed to its
death. It dies by the providence of God.
With Ferdinand the Seventh fell the Traditional Monarchy. With the flight of Isabella
the Second the Parliamentary Monarchy disappeared. With the renunciation of Don
Amadeo of Savoy the Elective Monarchy
falls. No one destroyed it. It died of natural
causes. Nobody has brought the Republic
into being. It is the creation of circumstances. It comes from a conjuncture of
Society and nature and history. Let us
salute it as the sun that rises by its own
gravitation on the horizon of our country."
17

With this final eloquent metaphor the discussion was closed, and the House proceeded to vote on the first part of the proposition. Two hundred and fifty-eight deputies voted for the adoption of the republican form of government; thirty-two against it. The result of the ballot having been proclaimed, Señor Figueras proposed that the result be at once communicated to the governor of Madrid, and to the authorities of the capital and province : that the same be telegraphed to the civil and military chiefs throughout the country, and that those foreign Governments with which Spain entertained friendly relations be advised of the change of her form of government.

The second proposition, which provided for the nomination of an Executive, to be named directly by the Assembly, was then approved without a division.

At a quarter-past nine the session was suspended for the purpose of informal consultation preparatory to voting on the organization of the Executive Power.

When at midnight the President again called the House to order, several deputies desired to record their votes in the affirmative on the proposition establishing a Republic.

The Presidency of the Republic was tendered to Señor Figueras, he having received two hundred and forty-four votes out of two hundred and fifty-six cast. Señor Castelar was appointed Secretary of State on a total of two hundred and forty-five votes; while Señor Pi y Margall, as Minister of the Interior, General Cordova as Minister of War, and the other members of the Government were elected by equally large majorities.

The Vice-President of the Chamber having announced the result, the members of the Government took their seats on the Ministerial bench amidst long continued cheering and applause.

The President of the Republic, rising to his feet, stated that he was unfitted to address the House owing to the moral and physical exhaustion he was experiencing after the anxieties of the last forty-eight hours. Oppressed by the immense responsibility laid upon him, he could only thank the Cortes for the confidence placed in him. For the present he could put forth no programme, but he declared that he and his colleagues were resolved that the approaching elections should be conducted with perfect regularity, and in accordance with the most ample liberty.

Thus terminated, at half-past two in the morning, one of the most eventful parliamentary sessions in Spanish history, and one of the most extraordinary political revolutions the world has ever witnessed.

With the exception of a momentary tumult in Seville, quickly and effectually suppressed, the transformation from the monarchical form of government to that of the republic had been accomplished without revolution—except in a parliamentary sense—without resorting to force, and without the shedding of blood. Within a few short months, however, the apparent calm was to be followed by a reactionary movement which again plunged the unhappy country in the vortex of insurrection and revolt, which, by a strange irony of Fate, was to yield in its turn to the triumphant reinstatement of the dynasty so ruthlessly banished in 1869.

With the fall of the Savoy Monarchy, and the creation of the Republic, our interest in Spanish political events must cease.

CHAPTER XV.

A FEW moments after six o'clock on the morning of February 12th, 1873, which day broke cold and rainy, four Court carriages could be seen issuing from the great portals of the Royal Palace, and slowly wending their way down the steep streets leading to the railway station.

In the first, accompanied by his wife, sat Amadeus I., elected by the People, through their representatives in the Constituent Cortes, to occupy the throne of Ferdinand and Isabella, of Charles the Fifth, and a host of glorious Sovereigns.

Convinced of the futility of further effort to achieve the pacification of the country by the establishment of his dynasty, and unwilling to play longer the part of a crowned intruder at the head of a mere political faction, Amadeus had returned the sceptre to those from whom he had received it, and now sought the freedom and liberty of action which, as Duke of Aosta, he could reasonably expect to enjoy.

Although Lisbon was the first stage of the journey it was now decided to undertake, the stay there would only be prolonged sufficiently to enable the Queen to regain her strength. Her Majesty, incompletely recovered from her recent confinement, was suffering from fever and exhaustion, as well as from the nervous shock caused by the exciting events of the past weeks. The medical council assembled at the Palace during the afternoon of the eleventh had agreed to allow their royal patient to undertake the long journey, fearing that even a temporary separation from her husband would, under the circumstances, do more harm than the unavoidable fatigue of travel. But they had given their consent with the utmost reluctance, fully realizing the danger of permanent injury to her health which would be run, and clearly foreseeing the development of the illness which in a few short years was to carry the distinguished sufferer to the tomb.

Even had the verdict of the physicians been adverse to the proposed journey, Amadeus was desirous of leaving the palace without delay. It was hinted that the royal family would occupy the Italian Legation until such time as the Queen could with safety undertake the journey. It was even said that Amadeus had declared to those around him that once his abdication accepted by the Cortes he became " ipso facto " a private citizen, and that as such, could he not at once leave Madrid, he would prefer to engage rooms in one of the hotels of the city.

Long before daybreak the inhabitants of the palace were astir, in fact the entire night had been passed by many in making hasty preparations for departure. In the ante-rooms were assembled those (few, alas !) who, faithful in adversity, desired to pay a last tribute of affection and respect to the masters they had learnt to love.

In the private apartments Señora de Madoz was assisting her royal mistress in her preparations for the journey. Before leaving her rooms the Queen, in taking leave of this faithful attendant, pressed upon her the breviary she always used, as well as various presents of great value.

At precisely six o'clock Don Amadeo, his wife and family, appeared. The Queen was carried in a sedan-chair, surrounded by her family and friends, and closely followed by a nurse bearing the infant Prince, scarcely a fortnight old. With their Majesties were Generals Tassara and Burgos, Count Rius, Señor Albareda, the King's aides-de-camp, and several others.

As the little procession advanced through the long suites of gorgeously decorated reception-rooms which had afforded so little satisfaction or pleasure to their late occupants, the servants and lower officials greeted them with expressions of respect and emotion. The soldiers of the Life Guard lined the great staircase, and rendered military honors. Amadeus appeared dejected, and with difficulty concealed his deep emotion, speaking hardly at all, and passing with eyes cast down ; the Queen wept bitterly as she was carried through the midst of those who had served her faithfully during her short sojourn in Spain. As the royal party passed the soldiers broke their ranks and followed on behind. Although some two hundred persons were thus gathered around their Majesties, an eye-witness states that no sound was audible. It seemed as if all present held their breath in order not to disturb the eloquent silence of what appeared to them a ceremony fraught with some mysterious religious import.

On reaching the portico at the foot of the stairs the bearers set down their burden, and Amadeus advanced and, lifting the Queen in his arms, tenderly placed her in the carriage which was in waiting. Señor Rivero here bade adieu to their Majesties, who earnestly charged him to watch over the interests of the servants they left behind them. To these Amadeus paid a full month's wages, besides making to each handsome and valuable presents, and asking them to retain possession of their liveries as souvenirs of their late master. A few moments later Maria Victoria gave the signal for departure, and the four carriages conveying the royal party and their suite, issued from the Prince's Gate and drove off in the direction of the Northern Station, where a special train had been in waiting since the night before.

During the short drive, as the carriages made their way through the Moro Gardens, the royal couple were greeted with cries of " Long live the King," by a small gathering of spectators, to which a rival group responded with shouts for the Republic. Beyond this no demonstration was made; and in fact the early hour and uncertainty of the King's movements prevented any considerable number of persons being present.

At the railway station the deputation appointed by the Assembly to accompany the King to the frontier was in waiting. It consisted of the Marquis de Seoane, Messieurs Montesinos, Moncasi, Rossell, Ulloa, Montero, Rios, Generals Tassara and Gandara, and others. Besides these gentlemen their Majesties were greeted on their departure by the Marquis de Sardoal, by the diplomatic representatives of Italy and Portugal, accompanied by their wives, the Italian Consul, and *five or six police agents*. Not a single Government official; not a single one of those who at the beginning of the reign had been so lavish in their protestations of friendship and loyalty; not even one of the recipients of the Queen's charities, or of those who had thronged her audience-chamber, and received of her royal bounty. Not even a Guard of Honor was furnished. It is true that Señor Rivero afterwards excused himself for this lack of courtesy by explaining that the necessary orders had been issued for the formation of a Guard of Honor, and an escort, but had mysteriously been countermanded.

The train provided for their Majesties consisted of a first-class carriage, in one of the compartments of which a bed had been prepared for the Queen; of a saloon-carriage for the deputation of Parliament and the suite, and of two second-class carriages for the soldiers who were to accompany the party, as well as of a couple of baggage-vans. The escort, however, being absent, these carriages remained vacant until the Southern Madrid station was reached, where Admiral Topete, and others in authority, arranged that the *eight policemen* in charge of the station should accompany the train in the capacity of escort.

With her babe, scarce a fortnight old, at her breast, and her two young children clinging to her knees, the unfortunate mother now started on the long and anxious journey across what had been her Kingdom, without any of the appliances for material comfort necessitated by her physical condition, while even the elementary wants of her children had been overlooked, or forgotten, in the hurry of departure. For long hours not a drop of milk or a cup of broth was obtainable.

Until Aranjuez was reached the stations through which the train passed were deserted; even here the crowd was small, and consisted mainly of those employed on the royal estate. A telegram from the Government had been received at Alcazar de San Juan, instructing the local authorities to greet the august travellers with the honors due their rank, and to furnish a more suitable escort than the eight police agents who had been unceremoniously picked up at Madrid. Here also some refreshments had been prepared in virtue of a telegraphic message dispatched from the train at Aranjuez. Descending from the carriage Amadeus opened himself a passage through the silent and respectful throng which crowded the platform, and seated himself at the table, where those who accompanied him also took places irrespective of rank or etiquette. The crowd, whose curiosity impelled them to stare at the late Chief of a nation of sixteen million souls, was so dense that the waiters had the utmost difficulty in serving those seated at table.

As the day wore on the crowds at the various stations increased; sometimes their Majesties were greeted with respect and sympathy, at others the hostility of the mob was undisguised. At Merida a firearm was discharged at the royal train, while on several occasions stones were thrown. At Badajoz the aspect of the crowd awaiting their Majesties was particularly threatening: here also the small escort was left as the train was shortly to enter Portuguese territory. Late at night the frontier was reached, and the train halted in front of the Custom-house. Amadeus here received the authorities, and took leave of those members of the Parliamentary Commission who had accompanied him thus far. At three o'clock in the morning the train again started for Lisbon, which was reached at a little after ten on the morning of the thirteenth.

Affectionately received by the Portuguese Sovereigns, by the representatives of Italy and Spain, and by the populace, the royal travellers were immediately conducted to the palace of Belem, where Maria Victoria found the rest she so greatly stood in need of.

"Thank God! Now I shall be able to live in peace!" had been the words uttered by the Queen when informed of the abdication.

Here in Lisbon she could at least have a foretaste of the peace and tranquillity her soul craved.

CHAPTER XVI.

AMADEUS had prepared Victor Emmanuel some time previous to its occurrence for the eventuality of his abdication, and had received in reply a message of emphatic disapprobation of the step he meditated. The King of Italy reminded his son that the destinies of a nation were not thus to be abandoned without weighty consideration, and that the people, in electing him their ruler, had confided to him sacred interests which were not lightly to be cast aside.

Uncertain as to the welcome he might expect in Italy, the Duke for a moment considered the advisability of establishing a temporary residence either in Belgium or Switzerland. However, when full details of the occurrences which had conduced to the abdication reached Italy, Victor Emmanuel changed his opinion, and hastened to extend a hearty invitation to his son to return to his native land, and at the same time dispatched the Italian frigate "Roma," to Lisbon to convey the royal couple to Genoa.

As was to be expected, the news of the King of Spain's abdication, and the causes which had prompted it, gave rise to much comment and controversy throughout Europe. By many the King was blamed for yielding in the face of difficulties which, although serious, might, it was argued, have been overcome by the exercise of a firm and decisive individual policy still strictly within the limits of the constitutional guarantees. By others again Amadeus was applauded for his discernment in appreciating the fact that his dynasty could never become popular with a considerable and increasing majority of his subjects, and for the unusual abnegation displayed in voluntarily sacrificing his crown, and the claims of his descendants, to what he conscientiously believed to be the best interests of his adopted country.

These latter were ready to agree with the

King when he exclaimed in weariness and
disgust :

" How can I be expected to succeed when
even those pledged to uphold and defend the
monarchy quarrel amongst themselves, and
sacrifice our mutual cause to personal ambitions ! "

By those who have perused the earlier
pages of this study, it will be remembered
that, from the moment of his arrival in Spain,
Amadeus had insisted, in his official speeches,
as well as in private conversation, that under
no circumstances would he impose himself, or
his dynasty, on the Spanish people. On four
occasions the Cortes had been dissolved and
fresh elections undertaken, and on each occasion the country had returned a more or
less substantial support to the Crown. It
was, however, extremely doubtful, owing to
the disturbed state of the Kingdom, and the
intrigues of contending political factions,
how far such elections really expressed the
national sentiment. As long and as often as
possible the King was kept in ignorance of
the true trend of public feeling ; or attempts
were made to warp his naturally sound judgment by garbled statements of political events
which it would have been well-nigh impos-

sible for him to personally verify. This treachery was perpetrated by those surrounding the throne: men whose personal ambitions passed before patriotic or loyal considerations, and who traded on the confidence reposed in them. It is doubtful, however, if even those nearest the King attached more than a passing significance to His Majesty's reiterated assertions concerning the limitations of his reign; while it is certain that the climax of February eleventh came as a surprise to many who considered themselves prepared for an eventual crisis.

Nor were the immediate reasons for the abdication either thoroughly or generally understood. Had the King decided to renounce the throne rather than affix his signature to a measure which he most earnestly disapproved, the opportuneness of his resolve would have been more readily comprehended; but having once signed the decree there would seem to have been no immediate reason for the step. That His Majesty should experience bitter disgust at having been practically entrapped into acquiescence by the adroitness of his ministers is natural, but was not generally accepted as sufficient ground for the extreme course adopted. His Majesty was at

18

liberty, it was urged, to dismiss his advisers and fill their places as he desired, and there were not wanting those who would have heartily supported such action. On the other hand, Amadeus had repeatedly affirmed that he would rule through the Cortes alone, and never antagonize the wishes of a majority in that body. By their adroit action in obtaining a vote of approbation and confidence in the Chamber, the Cabinet had isolated the Crown, and was in a position to defy it. The attempt on the part of the King to ignore such a vote and impose his views on the Chamber and Cabinet alike, necessitating, as it must, the dissolution of the Cortes should other counsellors accept office, would have been open to the interpretation of a coup-d'état.

We may regret the announcement of the abdication was not simultaneous with that of a refusal to sanction the proposed measure, but we must not hastily condemn an action imposed upon a constitutional ruler by his advisers and the voice of the people—as echoed through their legal representatives—alike.

In Italy the news of the King's departure from Madrid was received with dismay. General Lanza, then Italian Premier, telegraphing to Victor Emmanuel on February twelfth, says: "I understand Your Majesty's legitimate emotion in the presence of the grave and unexpected events in Spain. I am in consternation at possible political consequences. Spain torn by civil war will soon experience lamentable results and regret the withdrawal of the Prince who would have re-established order and prosperity. King Amadeus returns to Italy with greater fame; a most loyal, wise and courageous Prince. By his abdication the glory of the House of Savoy is not diminished but increased. He will undoubtedly receive an enthusiastic welcome in Italy, and his resolution and conduct will be applauded by all Europe." That Lanza was not as enthusiastic over the abdication as this official dispatch would lead us to believe has been demonstrated in a previous chapter describing, in the General's own words, his interview with the Duchess of Aosta on her return to Turin.

In spite of adverse criticism the general concensus of public opinion was that Amadeus had acted wisely. The German Press was inclined to see symptoms of French influence in the establishment of the republican form

of government in Spain, and was not slow
to attribute many of the difficulties encountered by the King to intrigues woven on the
other side of the Pyrenees, and not solely to
the Carlist leaders who were so unaccount-
ably permitted to use the north bank of the Bi-
dassoa as a base of operations. Gambetta's
organ, " La République Française," pronounced the spontaneous renunciation of the
" ardent and courageous Prince, a member of
the oldest reigning house in Europe, a most
rare act of intelligence and sentiment; a
deed, profoundly dignified and politic, un-
precedented in monarchical annals."

From Italy came hundreds of telegrams of
sympathy and admiration. " If you returned
to us flushed with victory," telegraphed Sena-
tor Imbriani, Syndic of Naples, " your name
would be far less glorious than it is to-day
after your magnanimous renunciation. . . .
You descend from the throne as you ascended
it—uncontaminated."

On February fifteenth the Italian Chamber
unanimously passed a resolution welcoming
the Prince should he decide to return to
Italy, the promoters of which were Signores
Marco Minghetti and Francesco Crispi.
" The Chamber of Deputies," so read the

resolution, " moved by the announcement of abdication of the King of Spain, being assured that it interprets the sentiments of the Nation, and recollecting that he fought for the Italian Fatherland, declares to the August Prince Amadeus that Italy will to-day receive him with even greater affection and devotion on account of admiration for his loyal, dignified and frankly constitutional conduct." Speaking in support of the resolution Signor Crispi added : " We all adhere to this motion. We were adverse to the acceptance of the Crown ; but to-day we are most glad, not for the unfortunate event to which it has led, but in noting that the Prince has chosen the best solution, that of abdicating a throne on which he could not reign in the name of Liberty."

Under date of March first, 1873, the Prince replied from Lisbon in the following terms :

" Mr. President :

" An arduous mission was offered me : I accepted it, making in so doing the greatest of sacrifices, that of my beloved Country. I accepted it in order to restore peace and tranquillity to Spain. Two years have now passed. I leave Spain more divided, more harassed than ever: with grief I confess it. Finding that Spain could not attain through me her happiness, I renounced the Crown, after having faithfully adhered to the constitution I had taken oath to. I am returning to Italy. You may be certain in finding in me a soldier, a lover of my Country, at whose service I place my life.

" I beg you, Mr. President, to be the interpreter of these sentiments to the Chamber of Deputies, as also of my most sincere thanks for the address they forwarded me.

" Accept, I request, the assurances of my highest esteem.

" AMADEUS OF SAVOY."

Speaking of his recent abdication to the members of a commission appointed by the City of Turin to offer His Royal Highness a Civic Crown (a gift of the highest symbolic distinction), on his return to his native city, Amadeus said: " Urged by public opinion, I accepted the Crown of Spain with the fallacious idea that, by faithfully observing the new constitution, my acceptance would restore to that noble people their ancient grandeur and prosperity. I am certain of having always done my duty and of having adopted all honest means of attaining that important object; but when I was convinced that my presence would become the pretext for even greater discord, I did not hesitate a moment, and I preferred to immediately vacate the throne."

Although it had been proposed to remain in Portugal only for the period strictly necessary for the Queen's convalescence, nearly three weeks elapsed before Her Majesty was in a fit condition to continue the journey. During this time the arrangements for the voyage to Italy were completed, and the Italian frigate " Roma " put in readiness to receive the royal travellers.

While greatly impressed by the events connected with his abdication, and especially by the attitude of the Provisional Government, and of the populace during his recent journey across Spain, Amadeus was not long in regaining his usual buoyancy of spirits, or in resuming his accustomed mode of life. That he had every right to be dissatisfied with the scant courtesy shown by the Provisional Government for his comfort or safety during the journey, even the Spanish papers freely admitted, qualifying the conduct of the King's former Ministers as "shameful and unworthy of gentlemen." Yet the Prince's nature was not one to long bear malice even towards those who at the beginning of his reign had so dramatically protested their resolve to die at the foot of the throne, should harm threaten their Sovereign.

A few days after the arrival of the Spanish Sovereigns the Diplomatic Corps accredited to the Portuguese Court made application for an audience. Although Amadeus declined to grant an official reception, he immediately signified his willingness to receive each member of the Diplomatic Corps individually and privately.

This evident disposition on the part of their late Ruler to discard all semblance or pretence of royal state, and his earnestly expressed desire to return, as completely as his birth and station would permit, to private life, caused general satisfaction in Spain, where there existed a nervous apprehension of foreign intervention, shared by many of those by whom the spontaneous and definite nature of the renunciation of the throne was but dimly comprehended.

To the impression, insidiously fostered by his enemies, that the King abandoned the country in order to seek and return with foreign aid, may be attributed in part the senseless hostile demonstrations made at many of the wayside stations through which the royal train had passed on its way to Portugal.

CHAPTER XVII.

On taking leave of their royal relatives, the
Duke and Duchess of Aosta, as they now preferred to be styled, together with their three
children, embarked on the " Roma," and set
sail for Italy.   The voyage was accomplished
without incident, and on March ninth the
frigate entered the harbor of Genoa, which
was gayly decorated with flags and bunting.

On landing their Royal Highnesses were received with every token of sympathetic affection and esteem on the part of their countrymen, who, with unfeigned spontaneity, welcomed not the dethroned Monarch, but the
fellow-citizen of whose conduct they were
proud.

By an almost unanimous vote of Parliament

the Royal prerogatives and appanages he had enjoyed before his acceptance of the Spanish Crown were restored to the Prince, and provision made for the resumption of his military rank. For reasons which were readily understood Amadeus desired for the present to reside quietly in Turin. Victor Emmanuel, although he greatly wished that his son should be near him, yielded to this earnestly expressed preference, which soon became a necessity on account of the increasingly delicate health of the Duchess.

The palace belonging to Maria Victoria having been let during their absence, the couple took up their residence on the ground floor of the royal castle at Turin, in a relatively small but comfortable apartment opening upon the beautiful gardens overhanging the Po. The rapid strides made by the disease which was gradually sapping the life of Maria Victoria soon made it advisable to move her to the Palace of Moncalieri, a great bleak pile situated within a few miles of Turin. In spite of the change of air the condition of the ex-Queen became daily more hopeless. Devotedly attended by her husband, who reserved to himself the performance of all the cares necessitated by her illness, the invalid was to be seen daily, while the weather was propitious, in the gardens of the palace. Unable to walk, or even stand upon her feet, the Duchess was usually wheeled about the grounds by Amadeus himself, accompanied by the little Princes, who romped and frolicked around their parents in all their childish carelessness and ignorant of their impending loss.

On November eighth, at San Remo, where she had been conveyed with the forlorn hope of benefit from the soft air, the Duchess breathed her last.

During the twenty-nine years of her eventful life Maria Victoria had tasted of triumphs calculated to inflame the passions of the least ambitious of women. With the exception of the Empress Eugénie we do not recollect a similar example in contemporaneous history. Yet to this truly womanly woman the glitter and splendor of a court were as nothing compared to the peace and happiness of her own fireside. Herself of noble birth she had become the wife of a Prince standing very near the throne, not as the result of any ambitious intrigue, but of a mutual passion which was not to be withstood. When later a crown was offered her she had reluctantly accepted

the irksome duties and responsibilities of her
new station, devoting her time and energies,
not to the display of the pomp and splendor
connected with her exalted rank, but in the
constant exercise of those charities and acts
of personal kindness which had become associated with her name long before any visions
of the royal purple had been raised before her
eyes. Totally devoid of worldly ambition
she had returned to private life with a feeling of intense relief. From a political point
of view her lack of ambition was, as has
already been stated, condemned by one of
Italy's foremost statesmen as detrimental to her
husband's interests ; but who shall say that
guided by her woman's finer intuition, she did
not more readily perceive and grasp from
the outset the subtle influences which made
the position of a foreign ruler in Spain an
anomaly ! An excessive political ambition
had a couple of years previously brought ruin
and misery to France : Maria Victoria preferred to be held responsible for an abdication
rather than a war. The democratic simplicity
of the Court at Madrid had been disagreeable
to many accustomed to the magnificence of
the old régime, but it should be recollected
that the Queen, as much by force of circum-

stances as from natural inclination, was obliged to restrict ceremony and ostentation to their narrowest limits. In this detail the Queen's action was profoundly politic, for although it might not meet with the views of the few, it could on the other hand give no offence to the masses who could reproach the sovereign with no lavish extravagances—save in her charities.

As a Queen Maria Victoria will be remembered for her care and tenderness of those in suffering or distress: as a Princess for her gracious dignity and great, though unobtrusive, learning and intelligence, which went hand in hand with all the purely domestic virtues of the wife and mother shared with her sisters in every social rank.

Participating in a sorrow which so deeply touched the Royal House, Parliament decreed to display the signs of mourning for a period of forty-five days.

"The mourning we adopt for her," said Signor Crispi, when proposing this mark of respect, " is a national mourning."

And as such it was considered by the Italian people; while in distant Spain the Prince's sorrow found a sympathetic echo in the hearts of those who had experienced the Queen's bounty, or had come within the sphere of her gracious influence.

The Duchess was laid at rest in the mausoleum of the members of the House of Savoy on the beautiful hill of the Superga, overlooking the city where the best years of her life's happiness had been spent, and the home whose dignified tranquillity she had so craved while seated on the glorious throne of Ferdinand and Isabella.

By Maria Victoria's express desire the ceremonial attending her burial was limited to the utmost simplicity compatible with her exalted rank. But besides the State officials, fulfilling the obligations of their various offices, the royal cortège was followed during the entire distance by thousands of poor and lowly mourners whose bearing testified to the wide-spread and genuine grief occasioned by the loss of their generous fellow-citizen.

The death of his wife was followed for Amadeus by a long period of terrible depression and of utter discouragement. Always strict in his religious observances the Prince now became fervently devotional. At this time the rumor was widely credited of his serious intention to abandon a world in which he had experienced such bitter deceptions and to seek the living death of the cloister. Little by little, however, the deep moral depression caused by his domestic misfortune gave way to the earnest appreciation of his public duties, and Amadeus began to devote himself passionately to military affairs, at the same time taking a personal share in the education and amusements of his children.

With the exception of trips to Paris, Baden Baden, Monte Carlo, and other places frequented by those in search of pleasure or distraction, the Duke continued to reside in Turin. To Rome he went but rarely, and only when his presence was necessitated by some official function, or business connected with family matters.

Shortly after the death of Maria Victoria the family had returned to the imposing Cisterna Palace, better known to-day as the Ducal Palace, and there established a permanent residence. An enthusiastic worshipper of the beautiful, and possessed of means amply sufficient to gratify his æsthetic tastes, Amadeus devoted much of his time to beautifying his home by the acquisition of pictures and works of art. At the same time an ardent devotee to sport, and lover of horseflesh, his stables were filled with specimens of the choicest breeds, and his purse always open for the encouragement of horsemanship both in his own country and abroad. In Turin his life was one of the greatest simplicity and freedom from constraint. Accompanied by his three young sons the Duke was accustomed daily to walk about the streets, stopping to admire the shop windows, and freely mingling with the busy crowds in the principal thoroughfares. Nor was it an unusual occurrence for him to enter one of the numerous cafés and, seating himself at one of the small marble tables, order his cup of coffee and smoke his cigar like any of the peaceful citizens who surrounded him. Although known to all, Turin soon learnt that Amadeus preferred to be recognized by none during these daily prowls and, consequently, with the exception of a respectful salute when unavoidably brought face to face, he was allowed to roam at pleasure unmolested by the offensive curiosity of the crowd.

But events were portending which were to modify the semi-private existence led by the ex-King, and once more bring his personality prominently before the public, although the stage on which he would now be called to

19

act his part must of necessity be considerably more restricted than that he had occupied in Spain.

In the opening days of 1878 two of the leading figures of the most active period of the Italian political renaissance were to disappear. Victor Emmanuel, the Father of Italian Unity, the first King of Italy, and Pius IX, the last Pope-King, within a few days of each other passed forever from the scene of their triumphs or misfortunes. Conqueror and Vanquished, each in his different sphere had been the idol, the mainspring of the creed they represented : each had fought valiantly for the standards they upheld, but for both the hour of personal activity had passed. Victor Emmanuel, now that the militant period of the unification was over, fretted at the tame constitutionalism and rasping etiquette imposed on the hero whose life had been spent on the battlefield, or midst the excitement of vital political issues. Pius IX. a self-constituted prisoner within the walls of his Ecclesiastical Palace, had lost in the eyes of the world at large the political significance he had maintained as a temporal ruler, and had acquired that of an awkward problem, although by no means a negligible

quantity, either to his conqueror or the rest
of Christendom. If the Monarch, amidst
the glorious results of a life of energy and
triumph, was weary of his Kingly trade, the
Pontiff may also be presumed to have experienced lassitude when in retrospect he contemplated the long series of humiliations and
deceptions to which he had been subjected,
and witnessed the growing indifference to
his political decadence manifested by thousands who had formerly applauded the " Papa
Re."

The news of the sudden death of Victor
Emmanuel, coming as it did out of a clear
sky, shook Italy to her foundations. The
greatness of the man could not be justly estimated during his lifetime, while even now,
at an interval of a score of years. his colossal
figure looms up in incomprehensible grandeur.
He is still too near to us for criticism—another
generation must pass before the magnitude
of his influence can be correctly focussed.
The idol of his people while he lived, he has
now become their Washington.

Amidst the consternation caused by the
death of this national hero, that of his vanquished rival, Pius IX., passed almost unper-
ceived. The Pope never dies is an axiom

which, like most axioms, must be interpreted according to the circumstances governing the case : the policy of the Vatican may never die, yet its success or failure may depend very largely on the characteristics of the man wearing the tiara at the moment its imposition is deemed expedient.   Where Pius IX. failed Leo XIII. might have succeeded.   The one swooned when informed of the decision of the Conclave; the same notification found the other fully equipped for the arduous task he was to undertake.   Given the same circumstances and opportunities, and who shall say what the result might have been had Leo XIII. occupied the Chair of St Peter from 1846 to 1878!

Amadeus of Savoy, Duke of Aosta.

Amadeus of Savoy, Duke of Aosta.

CHAPTER XVIII.

WHEN, on his accession to the Throne, King
Humbert for the first time opened the Italian
Parliament, Amadeus stood at his brother's
side. From this moment we find him prominently connected with public affairs and constantly employed in the service of his country.

By royal decree of January 27th, 1878,
Amadeus was placed in command of the
Seventh Army Corps, with headquarters in
Rome, and there he spent all the time
necessitated by his military duties, inhabiting
a small apartment in the east wing of the
Quirinal Palace. Humbert relied much on
the support and advice of his brother, while
the affection which had always closely bound
them became daily stronger.

As Crown Prince Humbert had had few opportunities of becoming known to the great majority of his future subjects, his military valor, exemplified by his conduct during the memorable episode at Villafranca in 1866, on which occasion he, in common with his brother, had run the greatest peril and covered himself with glory, was indeed a matter of history; but in politics he was inexperienced and unformed. The succession he was now called upon to take up was one of no common difficulty even for a politician versed in the art of the manipulation of men and parties. Much which had been overlooked, or condoned, in his father because he had made United Italy would be subject to carping criticism in his successor. The heroic phase of national unification was over, but Italy found herself in a transition stage, presenting political pitfalls and dangers scarcely less critical than those attending the actual conquests by force of arms of a former period. The process of assimilating and harmonizing the conflicting interests of a people hardly understanding the same language, and of widely differing customs, laws and usages, was to prove a tedious and perilous one. The south was jealous of the north: to the

Sicilian and the Neapolitan the Piedmontese
was almost a barbarian, and when his presence
was felt in the form of the tax-gatherer he
became uncommonly like an oppressor. If a
United Italy was to be the cause for increased
taxation, they had been better off under their
own Bomba. In the Eternal City the administrative branches of the Government were
far from feeling at home after a sojourn of
over seven years, while the colossal buildings
erected for the accommodation of the nation's
finances seemed indeed a hollow mockery.
Even the legislative sessions were marked
by demonstrations of petty opposition and
party intrigue wholly unworthy of the patriotism of those who had purchased at the cost of
noble sacrifice the opportunities now within
the nation's grasp.

A constitutional Monarch who is determined to scrupulously fulfil his duty is fet-
tered. His chains may be of gold, but they
are chains nevertheless. Amadeus had early
realized this in Spain, and Humbert was to
prove no exception to the rule. An individual policy unless seconded by ministers
and Parliament is of little account: the Sovereign must learn to rule through these, if
he is to rule at all. This the young King

quickly grasped, and with undaunted courage
set about his task, sacrificing personal inclination or preference to the duties of his position,
and the best interests of the nation.

With the death of Pio Nono and the advent of Leo XIII., the struggle with the
Vatican entered upon a new phase which
must be met with weapons adapted to neu-
tralize the tactics of that cunning foe : the
more to be dreaded by reason of the insidious methods employed to prejudice the judgment of the multitudes blindly accepting
a guidance not purely spiritual, and a juris-
diction not merely moral. Nor was Italy
alone to suffer from the effects of a policy
which aimed at the very foundation of her
future being, namely, the education of her
youth. Germany with the Culturkampf,
England with her Irish question, the United
States, Spain, France, in a word the civilized
world, were to feel, in one degree or another,
the tremendous power still wielded by the
humble prisoner from behind the walls of his
stronghold.

During the next twelve years Amadeus
was the *alter ego* of the King : the trusted
confidant and counsellor ; the deputy who,
by virtue of his exalted rank, was employed

on missions of such nature as were beyond
the sphere of an ordinary ambassador. As
such we hear of him at the Courts of Berlin,
St. Petersburg, London and Lisbon. With
his appointment as Inspector-General of the
Army in 1879 his military duties became still
more engrossing, while in addition to his
labors as a soldier those scarcely less arduous pertaining to his royal rank made frequent demands and inroads upon his privacy.
In spite of these the Prince insisted upon
making his home in Turin whence, when
necessity compelled, he would journey to the
utmost limits of the Kingdom to return
again, once the duty accomplished, to his beloved fireside.

It was during one of these sojourns in his
native city that, in September, 1884, the news
reached Amadeus of his brother's determination to visit his cholera-stricken subjects in
Naples. The Prince read the telegram announcing the King's impending departure
for the south in a newspaper purchased during a stroll through the streets. Glancing
at his watch, he discovered that he had exactly
the requisite time to reach the railway station
before the departure of the next express for
Rome.

As he jumped into the first cab he found he cried out to those in his company at the time: "I am off to Naples with His Majesty. If there is a danger to be faced my place is at his side."

On this occasion the Prince's luggage consisted of the walking-stick he carried in his hand.

Early on the morning of the eighth Amadeus reached Rome, and a couple of hours later the train bringing the King entered the station. The greeting between the brothers was full of affectionate tenderness: each was secretly proud of the other, yet each refrained from expressions of surprise or admiration. On the platform Signor Depretis, at that time Italian Prime Minister, also awaited the King, and announced that, in spite of his advanced age (he was then nearly seventy), he desired to take part in the journey to Naples. The railway station was surrounded by an immense crowd which had gathered to testify to the universal admiration the King's conduct gave rise to in the Capital. Cheer after cheer thundered forth when, at a few minutes after nine o'clock, the King and Amadeus entered the train, which slowly steamed out of the Roman station on its way to the plague-infested south. A continual ovation greeted the Sovereign as he passed the wayside stations on his noble errand of charity and devotion.

At four o'clock the same afternoon Naples was reached. Here the royal travellers were received with frantic demonstrations of affectionate loyalty : the cries of " Long live Humbert," " Long life to Amadeus," acted like strong drink on the multitudes who awaited their Sovereign as they might have awaited the Redeemer. Men and women wept as they beheld the royal brothers drive through the streets ; some knelt as they passed, as they knelt when the sacred images were displayed at Piedigrotta, and invoked the blessings of Heaven on the head of the " Second Father of his Country," as Naples now styled Humbert. Amidst the wildest enthusiasm the royal equipages made their way to the Palace, in front of which the wild tumult reached the highest pitch of frenzied devotion.

In various quarters of the town, inhabited by the most ignorant and squalid classes of the population, the sanitary measures carried out, or prescribed by the municipal authorities, had given rise to dogged opposition or

open revolt.   The miserable populace refused
to abandon the foul dens in which they lived,
or to cease drinking the polluted water of
the wells into which all the filth and abom-
inations of the neighborhood filtered.   Before this fierce fanaticism the resources of
science were powerless, while in the face of
threatened expulsion the living rose to defend
their putrid dead, themselves in turn falling
easy victims to their senseless bigotry.   In
vain had the doctors struggled against this
idolatry of filth : in vain had the Cardinal-
Archbishop himself exhorted the people to
obey the decrees issued by the sanitary com-
missions ; it was by force alone that any
attempts at sanitation could be accomplished.

Naturally enough many of those whose
circumstances permitted had sought safety
from the fell disease in flight; it is worthy
of record, however, that several members of
the highest aristocracy remained in their
homes to render what assistance they could,
while the conduct of the Government and
municipal officials was in many instances
subject of admiration throughout the length
and breadth of Italy.

In the course of the day after their arrival

Humbert and Amadeus, accompanied by the faithful members of their respective staffs, by Signor Depretis, His Eminence the Cardinal-Archbishop Sanfelice, and others, began their inspection of the hospitals, temporary shelters, and sanitary arrangements. On these missions of mercy His Majesty insisted on being initiated into every detail of the work in hand. Day after day the two brothers walked side by side amongst the horrors of the plague-stricken city, bringing relief to those to whom relief was still possible, and consolation and sympathy to the poor wretches beyond the reach of human aid. With words of praise and encouragement they urged on the unselfish workers in the congested districts, where the dead and dying lay side by side amidst the loathsome filth and sickening stench of nameless poverty. In their daily rounds of the hospitals they paused at every bed, promising the victims of the deadly scourge that their dear ones should be provided for, and soothing the agonies of the doomed. To the widows and orphans sheltered in the hastily-constructed tenements to which they were conveyed after the destruction of their pestilential dens, the King and Amadeus came in the light of a Providence to which they clung with the tenacity of utter despair and helplessness.

The moral effect of the Sovereign's visit was excellent, and reacted on the vitality of a naturally careless population, easily cast down but equally prompt in its recuperative forces once the stimulus given. The plague was raging furiously on the arrival of the royal brothers, and the death-roll reached its maximum on the second day of their stay in Naples; from that date, with occasional oscillations, it began gradually to decrease. Although this diminution in the mortality returns must be attributed in great part to the change of temperature, the value of the King's example in stimulating the exertions, not only of the officials but of the people themselves, to trample out the scourge, should not be under-estimated.

In spite of the entreaties of those around him, His Majesty refused to entertain any suggestion of departure until a decided and undoubted improvement in the sanitary conditions of the province should have taken place. To those who urged exaggerated precautions for his personal safety, he replied that while he would not willingly lay himself open to infection, yet his first duty being

the care of his stricken subjects, his intercourse with those most in need of his aid
must not be interfered with. Nor would
the King passively accept official reports
concerning the condition of certain hospital
wards, or quarters of the city; but insisted,
often to the chagrin of those responsible, on
a personal inspection of every detail.

To Baron Nicotera, who was especially
urgent and diligent in advancing reasons
of state for extraordinary precautions and
immediate departure, Humbert smilingly
retorted:

"Do you, who have been Minister of the
Interior, thus interpret individual liberty?
There is room for us all here in Naples."

Finally, on September fourteenth, the situation had so much improved that the royal
party again started on the journey north.
Before leaving Naples the King handed the
Syndic the sum of three hundred thousand
francs (sixty thousand dollars) to be used in
giving aid to those incapacitated by illness,
and for the relief of orphans left destitute
and homeless.

Meanwhile thousands of telegrams and
congratulatory addresses had poured in:
every city in Italy testified to its admiration

of the noble self-denial of the royal brothers, and of the courage of the officials who had accompanied then in their daily rounds. Turin prepared to give the Prince a welcome worthy of the son she was so justly proud of. The national exposition he had done so much to promote and encourage was about to close, and the usual population of the city was increased by thousands drawn thither by its manifold attractions; the opportunity was consequently exceptional.

When Amadeus descended from the train at Turin, he found the station and adjacent streets one solid mass of fellow-citizens and visitors flocked hither to do him honor. As each group caught a glimpse of the heroic Prince the frantic cheers redoubled, and the popular enthusiasm increased at every step.

Hardly had the carriage slowly passed out from the station yard when a terrific crash silenced the hearty greetings of the crowd. A portico of masonry in course of construction had suddenly collapsed at the very moment the royal carriage passed before it, and buried in its fall the five workmen at work at the time. With a cry of horror Amadeus sprang from the carriage and rushed to the scene of disaster, which he was the first to reach. With his own hands he began tearing away the débris in the hope of releasing the unfortunate victims. In vain was his attention called to the dangerous state of the walls still standing; until the last man was rescued the Prince refused to leave the spot.

As well may be imagined, this dramatic incident, affording ocular proof of the courageous energy of the man they had come forth to welcome, gave rise to a scene of popular enthusiasm which defies description. The Prince's carriage was taken by assault by those eager to grasp his hand and give utterance to the admiration they felt for their fellow-citizen who, having but just turned his back on dangers incurred while ministering to those afflicted by a terrible epidemic, did not hesitate a moment to face the peril of tottering walls In the attempt to rescue the lowly victims of a prosaic building accident in his native city.

The military duties assigned to Amadeus had proved no sinecure, and had indeed demanded his close and constant attention. This the Prince accorded ungrudgingly, for his heart was in his work, and he possessed the true soldierly pride in the advancement and efficiency of military science and organiza-

20

tion. With her admission into the alliance already existing between Germany and Austria (henceforth to be known as the Triple Alliance), Italy had assumed the military and naval obligations and responsibilities of a first-class Power. The constantly recurring scare of French intervention, in ecclesiastical afairs, or even an invasion to restore the temporal power, had led, on the part of Italy, to the cultivation of intimate relations with the two great central Powers. The financial and commercial wisdom of the adhesion, which was to irrevocably alienate French sympathies may be questioned: politically it must be looked upon as no mean factor in the long series of peaceful years enjoyed by the great European nations. Nevertheless the demands imposed by the obligations she was forced to assume have cost Italy sacrifices of the most onerous kind, while they have taxed her resources to the utmost limits of endurance. The injuries done her material prosperity by the rupture of amicable commercial relations with France have not been counterbalanced by any great financial advantages in other quarters, or even been attended by the equivocal compensation of glorious feats of arms. To the great mass

of Italians the Austro-Prussian alliance was
not merely distasteful but antipathetic and
frankly incomprehensible. For generations
the Austrian had been held up to them as
the embodiment of their bitterest foe—an oppressor; a hated tyrant; whose destruction
was to be encompassed by every means at
their disposal. Now they were told that their
salvation lay in cultivating the closest political and social relationship with that country,
and with another Teutonic nation which in
their ignorance they confounded with their
late enemy. Villafranca had been a bitter
pill to swallow, while the cession of Nice and
Savoy had opened many previously blinded
eyes concerning the disinterestedness of
French friendship. But to the former there
had at least been a golden coating of military
glory, while even the latter had had some "semblance of plausibility" in the affinity of language and origin. The strength of the political advocates of the new alliance lay in their
fidelity to the Crown, and the most cherished
of national conservative institutions. Those
loudest in their denunciations of the Austro-
Germanic compact were advowedly anti-dy-
nastic in their home politics: to a great extent agitators whose professed sympathies

with their Latin sister were prompted rather
by her republican form of government than
by any considerations of blood-relationship.
To these the prime object of a French alliance
was the introduction and fostering of French
radical institutions of the most advanced and,
naturally, anti-clerical type.

A different feeling existed in military
circles, even amongst those uninfluenced by
political considerations. By virtue of this
alliance the Italian officer became a partner
of the most military nation in Europe, whose
legions had but recently won the admiration
and applause of the civilized world. Professional pride was stimulated to the utmost,
and an incalculable impetus given to military
affairs throughout the Kingdom, by which
the reorganization and remodelling of both
branches of the service became topics of absorbing interest in parliamentary debate as
well as in the military clubs.

Martial enthusiasm was further intensified
by the recently inaugurated policy of African
colonial extension. The opportunity lost at
Tunis was to be amply atoned for by the development of Massaua and expansion of
Erithrea. In spite of the disaster of Dogali,
or perhaps on account of it, official enthusi-

asm for Abyssinian conquest was inflamed to fever heat, yet this again was purely professional; the occupation of Massaua was a political and military achievement; as a colonial enterprise it was from the first a distinct failure. The Italian emigrant continued to prefer expatriation in the Argentine, or United States, to the comparatively thankless soil and extreme climate of the Red Sea province, and this notwithstanding the substantial inducements temptingly dangled before his eyes by Government or private agencies. On the other hand, the native population of the new colony had little or nothing to offer in exchange for the products of Italian manufacturing industries. Whatever riches the newly baptized Erithrea had formerly possessed had died with the suppression of the slave-trade, and the divergence of caravan-commerce into new channels. But as a school of war its value was considerable. To the student of military science in search of an opportunity for the practical application of theoretical tactics it offered a field of operations not to be despised. In quarrels with neighboring tribes, and later with the Negus himself, it certainly afforded Italian Generals experiences—not universally agreeable, however—which they would have sought in vain on the parade-ground, or field of manœuvres at home. The difficulties encountered for the rapid transportation of large bodies of troops by sea and land, together with the organization and maintenance of a vast commissariat in a distant and almost uninhabited country, were met with an efficiency and promptness which was subject for congratulation and just pride.

As Inspector-General of the Army, and later as Inspector General of Cavalry, Amadeus had in no mean degree contributed to the reorganization and military education of the national forces. The latter appointment had proved most congenial to the Prince, whose predilection for that arm was well-known. The duties were onerous, necessitating frequent expeditions to the various garrisons of the Peninsula, but these he never failed to fulfil with a conscientious regularity hardly to be expected of one whose manifold social and political duties might have been presumed to occasionally clash with the strict observance of military discipline.

When not on active service Turin remained the Prince's headquarters. Continuing the noble example set by Maria Victoria, Amadeus interested himself in the charitable institutions of the city and environs, and personally superintended the disbursement of his donations. It was not only the institutions for the relief of the poor and destitute which bore witness of the Prince's unflagging bounty; many a member of some noble family fallen into decay, scores of humble employees in momentary pecuniary embarrassment, were tided over their difficulties by the timely generosity of their royal patron: many an officer's widow, or the orphans of a soldier, owed the little comforts of life denied them by their narrow pensions, to the kindness of a heart never hardened to the appeals of sorrow and distress. In most cases some investigation was made of the circumstances which led to the application, but in many others the mere application for aid was considered sufficient by the Prince, who held the theory that it was better to be occasionally deceived by an unworthy petitioner than to turn away real distress for the want of proper credentials.

CHAPTER XIX.

AT Moncalieri, hard-by, in the huge barrack-like palace where Victor Emmanuel I. died in 1824, and where Amadeus himself had spent much of his childhood during the reign of Charles Albert, and the early years of the eventful rule of Victor Emmanuel II., lived the Duke's eldest sister, the Princess Clotilde.

Married in 1859 to Prince Jerome Bonaparte, cousin of the Emperor Napoleon the Third, not from inclination but as the result of the famous Plombière's interview between the Emperor and Count Cavour, the Princess's life had for years been one of bitter deception and disappointment. The gay existence of the Tuileries had never appealed to the daughter of the House of Savoy, accustomed from infancy to the duties and stern responsibilities of power rather than the brilliancy and glamour it carried in its train. These views, combined with a rather austere exterior and unyielding reserve, had not contributed to any personal success of the young bride at the Court of her Imperial cousin. Prince Jerome, while possessing to a marked degree brilliancy of intellect, was lacking in the amiable qualities indispensable for popularity, while his misplaced jealousy often brought him politically in open antagonism with the Emperor.

Under these circumstances, and the wide divergence of their views on religious questions, the union was hardly calculated to contribute to the domestic happiness of either party. Holding the convictions she held, the occupation of Rome, and the policy of the Italian Government in regard to the Vatican, were blows from which her religious conscience never rallied.

After the fall of the French Empire the family of Prince Jerome had resided principally on their beautiful estate of Prangins, on the Lake of Geneva, but on the death of Victor Emmanuel the Princess had returned to Italy, and made her home in Turin. Her two sons, Prince Victor and Prince Louis, were naturally much from home, but Princess Lætitia, her only daughter, resided almost continuously with her mother.

During his frequent visits to Moncalieri Amadeus was very dependent on the society of his niece, the charming Princess Lætitia, and, in spite of the relationship and difference of age, a warm attachment sprang up between them. The idea of a marriage was at first received with great repugnance by the members of the royal family, but the Prince's determination finally overcame all opposition, and the union was solemnized in Turin on September 11, 1888. On this occasion the Prince's younger sister, Maria Pia, Queen of Portugal, together with the King, her husband, and the members of the Houses of Savoy and Bonaparte, assembled in Turin, lending by their presence special magnificence to an event which was characterized by much ceremony and pomp.

On the 22d of June of the following year the young Duchess of Aosta was delivered of a son, who received the name of Humbert, and on whom his uncle bestowed the title of Count of Salemi, in commemoration of the decree, signed by Garibaldi and Crispi in the

Princess Laetitia Bonaparte, Dowager Duchess of Aosta.

Princess Laetitia Bonaparte, Dowager Duchess of Aosta.

town of that name in 1866, proclaiming the national unity under the sovereignty of the Savoy Dynasty.

During the summer of 1889 the Prince was troubled almost continuously with a cough which, greatly to his annoyance, he found it impossible to completely shake off. In spite of this ailment he continued to occupy himself with military duties, frequently exceeding arduous, without the least care or thought of his physical condition. On the death of his brother-in-law, the King of Portugal, in October of the same year, it became necessary for Amadeus to attend the funeral ceremonies as the deputy of his royal brother. The journey, combined with the painful nature of his errand, greatly taxed his strength, which was still further undermined by attacks of intermittent fever. Heedless of all advice, the Prince continued to ride out in all weathers, frequently returning home drenched to the skin, and racked by the persistent cough.

Notwithstanding his obvious physical unfitness, Amadeus started in December for Caserta to inspect the cavalry regiments quartered there. On the day after his arrival the Prince passed nine hours on horseback, in a continuous deluge of rain, and returned to the hotel where he had established his residence, thoroughly drenched and shivering with cold. The same evening, during a dinner to which had been invited several of the officers in command, Amadeus was seized with such a violent paroxysm of coughing that he was obliged to leave the table.

Although on his return to Turin the Prince did his best to conceal or make light of his condition, it was apparent to those about him that he suffered considerably. For months past it had seemed as if his very nature had undergone some mysterious change : he so universally cheerful now appeared morose ; he whose kind word and gay jest was proverbial had of late become peevish and irritable in his intercourse with those who approached him. And especially was this ill-humor noticed when any reference was made in his presence to his altered state of health, or when the most ordinary precautions were suggested.

At last the day came when Amadeus could fight no longer against the terrible foe whose hand was on his throat. On January 13th, 1890, he consented to put himself under the doctor's care, and take to his bed. Once his head on the pillow his old serenity of manner seemed to return.

"Life is a voyage," he exclaimed as he settled himself. "I have done with travelling," he added a moment later. Words which he repeated on the last day of his life, scarcely a week later.

Although no serious consequences were at first anticipated, the pneumonia, for such it proved to be, rapidly assumed an intensity which justified the greatest anxiety. The news spread quickly throughout Turin causing general consternation, while Italy and all Europe anxiously followed the progress of the disease in one who, although his hour of celebrity had been brief, yet had always occupied an exalted position on the stage of political events, and whose close proximity to a throne placed him in the foremost rank.

On January seventeenth, the bulletin, issued by Doctors Bacelli, Bruno, Gamba, Bozzolo and Turletti, announced that the general weakness of the patient had increased, and that the Prince's condition must be considered most serious.

A little before noon on the same day Cardinal Alimonda, Archbishop of Turin, personally visited the Prince, and administered the Sacrament.

The news that the Prince had received the last consolation of the Church spread like wild-fire through the astounded city, and the streets adjacent to the Ducal palace were quickly thronged by thousands of sympathizers from all classes of society. Hour by hour official bulletins were issued, and, passing through the expectant crowd, were rapidly disseminated, not only in the city and suburbs, but throughout the length and breadth of Italy.

At the first alarm King Humbert hurriedly left the capital, and travelled as fast as steam could carry him to the bedside of his beloved brother. At every station where a stop was necessary telegrams were handed His Majesty, each of which held out fainter promise that he could arrive in time. As a last resource the doctors in attendance administered oxygen in the hope that life might be prolonged at least sufficiently to permit the Prince to embrace once more his royal brother, and to this end the patient harbored every particle of his failing strength.

Finally, at one o'clock on the afternoon of the eighteenth, the train drew up in the Turin station, and the King sprang to the platform, where his brother-in-law, the Duke of Genoa, was in waiting. Hastily greeting the local authorities assembled to welcome the sovereign, Humbert, accompanied by the Duke, entered a carriage and was rapidly driven to the Cisterna Palace. As he passed through the silent crowds which lined the streets, His Majesty's face wore a look of such intense anguish that it brought tears to the eyes of many a spectator. The royal carriage was received in the court-yard of the palace by the Prince's young sons, the Duke delle Puglie and Count of Turin. Embracing his nephews the King at once made his way to the sick-room where, to his intense relief, he found his brother still conscious and able to speak,

" See," he faintly murmured as he held the hand he loved so well, " I have allowed the doctors to torment and torture me, and have taken everything they prescribed, in order to be enabled to enjoy the supreme consolation of expiring in your arms."

The King, choking with suppressed emotion, affectionately endeavored to encourage the sufferer with words of cheerful optimism :

" No, dear Humbert," sighed the Prince,

"it is now only a question of hours ; but I die happy, having been permitted to embrace you once again."

Turning to Princess Clotilde Amadeus asked to be given the crucifix which hung over his bed. Kissing the image, and handing it to his wife to kiss, he gently besought her that when he was gone it should be placed between his folded hands. To his brother he confided those dear to him, while he urgently charged those around him with affectionate messages for his third son, Prince Louis, Duke of the Abruzzi, at that moment on service on a frigate in South American waters. Of the King he requested that his farewell greetings be conveyed to his comrades in arms.

His mind seemed at this time particularly clear and active, especially when he gave some directions concerning the funeral ceremonies, which he desired should be of a military character, and as simple as circumstances would permit. He expressed strong aversion to having his remains embalmed, or that they should be suffered to lie in state.

At half-past five the Prince's condition appeared more easy, and those present withdrew into the adjoining room in order that he might rest more quietly.

An hour later, however, they were hastily re-assembled round the bed, for the death-agony had begun.

At ten minutes to seven on the evening of January eighteenth Amadeus breathed his last in the arms of King Humbert.

By order of the King, Count Balbo, Grand Master of the Ducal Household, immediately left the death-chamber and communicated the sad news to the Captain of the Guard, who in turn informed the crowds thronging the streets leading to the palace. Thus from mouth to mouth the tidings spread rapidly over the city, bringing mourning and grief to all classes of the population.

To the Syndic and Prefect, who arrived simultaneously at the palace, the King, weeping bitterly, exclaimed: "I have lost my dearest and most sturdy support; the trusted and devoted counsellor from whom my heart had no secrets."

The death was at once officially communicated to Signor Crispi, then Prime Minister; and through Count Giannotti, Grand Master of the Royal Court, a statement transmitted to the Diplomatic corps and state officials.

Next morning the walls of the city were covered with the Syndic's notification to the in-

21

habitants : "Fellow-citizens; " it read, " A great misfortune has overtaken the Royal Family and the nation.   Yesterday at 6 : 50 P.M. His Royal Highness, Prince Amadeus, Duke of Aosta, departed this life.   The mourning of the Royal Family is mourning for Turin—is the mourning of Italy.   Turin mourns a well-loved Prince : one of whom his native city was proud.   The nation deplores the loss of the valorous soldier who shed his blood in the battles for her independence ;—he who on the throne of a powerful Kingdom exemplified the traditional loyalty of the House of Savoy ; —who was the faithful companion of his August Brother wherever a peril to be faced, or a sorrow in need of consolation, called the Sovereign amongst his people.   In great afflictions there is consolation in community of affections.   In these days of national grief the inhabitants of Turin feel more deeply the indissoluble bonds of love and devotion which for centuries have united them to the glorious dynasty—and trust that the grief of the King, of the Royal Family, of the August Consort, and sons of the Prince, may be relieved by the certitude that in grateful Italian hearts the memory of Amadeus of Savoy will live forever."   The   sentiments   expressed   in the above-quoted document were sincerely echoed by the population. On all sides were to be seen tokens of mourning ; even the houses of the very poor being decked with lowly symbols of woe, touching in their naïve simplicity, but illustrating most eloquently the universal sorrow.

To those in the Palace the etiquette which, even in the midst of death and sorrow, hedges exalted rank, brought fresh cause for suffering. Privacy, the refuge and inestimable boon of individual grief, is denied to the wearer of a crown, and King Humbert, despite his breaking heart, found himself obliged to receive delegations or listen to long addresses of official condolence which left little time for the indulgence of personal sorrow.

On the evening of the nineteenth, however, the King, summoning the Princes Emmanuel and Victor, the late Duke's eldest sons, entered the chamber of death. Declining all assistance, and banishing all others from the room, the King and his two young nephews gently lifted the body from the bed, and with their own hands laid it in the coffin, covering the remains with violets and pure white flowers. Here, beyond the reach of

any official eye, they bade an eternal farewell to the brother and father they had loved
so well.

At noon on the twentieth, the Queen, accompanied by the Prince of Naples, reached
Turin from Rome. The King met Her
Majesty at the railway station, surrounded
by the Duchess of Genoa, Prince Louis
Napoleon, his nephew, Signor Crispi, the
ladies and gentlemen in waiting, and all the
State, Court and Municipal officials. An immense but silent crowd lined the principal
approaches to the station. As the train drew
up at the platform Humbert advanced to the
door of the Queen's compartment, and, aiding
Her Majesty to descend, tenderly embraced
her. Arm in arm the royal couple, dressed
in deepest mourning, passed through the
bareheaded crowd, gravely acknowledging
the respectful salutations offered on all sides,
and entering the carriage in waiting were
driven to the Palace where the widowed
Duchess received them.

On the morning of January 22, Turin was
early astir. From all quarters of the city
groups of sight-seers streamed into the principal thoroughfares, there to take up advantageous positions to view the funeral proces-

sion. Commerce was at a standstill—not only the shops in the streets through which the procession must pass being closed, but even those in the distant and poorer districts. Throughout the long, straight streets the windows and balconies were draped in black : below soldiers lined the sidewalks, hedging in the silent crowds patiently waiting to offer a last salute to their Prince.

At ten o'clock the booming of cannon announced the formation of the procession, and half an hour later the march began, opened by bodies of troops and civic delegations. An officer on horseback carrying the Prince's sword preceded the hearse. The coffin rested on a gun-carriage drawn by eight horses, and was followed by the Prince's favorite charger, led by two grooms, one on either side. Immediately behind walked the King, clad in the full dress uniform of a General, with the Duke delle Puglie on his right and the Count of Turin on his left. A few paces separated the chief mourners from the Prince of Naples, Duke of Genoa, Prince of Hohenzollern and Prince of Sweden, who were in turn closely followed by the high dignitaries of the State and Court, representatives of Army and Navy, and distinguished delegates of various ranks and professions. Behind these again came six funeral cars, each drawn by six horses caparisoned in black and silver, and laden with the innumerable floral wreaths sent from all parts of Italy and Europe.

On the arrival of the procession at the Church of the Gran Madre di Dio, the coffin was carried to the high altar where the religious ceremonies were performed and the absolution given. These rites being concluded, the King, Prince of Naples, Duke of Genoa, and the late Prince's two elder sons, proceeded to the Superga there to await the arrival of the remains and assist at the final ceremonies and sealing of the vault.

The great dome of the basilica had not been decorated—only the high altar was draped and lighted by a profusion of tall wax-candles. Before it a low catafalque was prepared on which the coffin was to rest during the performance of the last rites. The crypt, where the members of the Royal Family are buried, was carpeted in black, and bare, save for a small table provided with a silver ink-stand, two goose-quills, and a couple of sticks of black sealing-wax. From the ceiling hung silver lamps which shed a subdued light over the simple but impressive funeral monuments.

The Queen and widowed Duchess entered the basilica a few moments before the arrival of the coffin which was conveyed up the steep incline on a gun-carriage drawn by six horses mounted by artillerymen. Shrouded in the folds of the Italian flag the coffin rested before the high altar. On it lay the decorations, helmet and sword of the deceased. Of the hundreds of wreaths only three now accompanied the remains: those sent by the King and Queen, the widow and sons, and Prince Louis, who was mourning his father far away on the South American coast.

On the conclusion of the final short religious service the coffin was carried to the crypt and placed in the vault adjoining that in which rested Maria Victoria. Here Count Balbo read the burial certificate, copies of which, after being signed in triplicate by those present, were deposited in the respective archives of the basilica and of the Court, both in Turin and Rome.

Two masons now stepped forward and walled up and sealed the vault, placing in position the tablet bearing the inscription of which the following is the translation :

H. R. H. Amadeus of Savoy, Duke of Aosta.

Born in Turin, May 30, 1845. Died there January 18, 1890.

THE END.